A Dark Shadow's Kill

Bob Doerr

Jim West mystery/thriller™ Book 11

TotalRecall Publications, Inc.
1103 Middlecreek
Friendswood, Texas 77546
281-992-3131   281-482-5390 Fax
www.mousegate.com

Copyright © 2025 by: Bob Doerr
All rights reserved
ISBN: 978-1-64883-398-4
UPC: 6-43977-43984-0

Library of Congress Control Number: 2025942192

FIRST EDITION
1   2   3   4   5   6   7   8   9   10

This is a work of fiction. The characters, names, events, views, and subject matter of this book are either the author's imagination or are used fictitiously. Any similarity or resemblance to any real people, real situations or actual events is purely coincidental and not intended to portray any person, place, or event in a false, disparaging or negative light.

This book is dedicated to my wife, Leigh.
She has been my inspiration that has gotten me
this far in my writing and most of the other things
I have accomplished.
The journey would never have been this great
without you.

Award Winning Author: Bob Doerr

 grew up in a military family, graduated from the Air Force Academy, and had a career of his own as a Special Agent in the Air Force Office of Special Investigations (OSI). His education credits include a Masters in International Relations from Creighton University. His 28 plus years in the military sent him to 18 foreign counties and all over these United States. A full-time author, he has twenty-three published books. Bob was selected by the Military Writers Society of America in 2013 as its Author of the Year. He is an Eric Hoffer Award winner and several of his books have won medals in other competitions. Bob lives in Garden Ridge, TX, with his wife of 52 years and their ornery cat Cinco.

About The Book

This book keeps Jim close to his home in Clovis, New Mexico. Jim's peaceful morning is disrupted by Jessica Perez, a teenager, who arrives at his house unannounced, asking for his help in locating her missing mother. Jim reluctantly agrees to help, while hoping the police will ask him to stay out of their investigation. The police tell Jim their investigation has hit a dead end and suggest he take a rookie deputy out to the Jessica's home to see if they can come up with any new ideas. While they are talking to the daughter at her home near Melrose, NM, the young deputy gets a call that sends Jim and the deputy to a remote location where a woman's body has been found. The investigating takes a new turn and more murder victims start turning up. Information is slowly developed indicating one or more killers are looking for something and killing anyone in their way. Jim and the authorities soon realize that the killers will not leave any stone left unturned, and Jessica may be that last stone.

A Dark Shadow's Kill
is the eleventh book in the Jim West mystery/thriller series.

Chapter 1

Anita Perez cursed herself for not putting on her shoes before coming out to find her cigarettes. She had parked her ancient Dodge Caravan on the mostly gravel parking spot near the back door, but the weeds here in the high plains of New Mexico were nothing if not tenacious. Rather than grab the pack of cigarettes and dash back in, she sat on the driver's seat, doing her best to pull a nasty sand burr out of the sole of her left foot.

While she tugged carefully at the burr, she saw the small trees off to the side of the house light up from the headlights of a vehicle. After a few seconds, she could hear the engine as the vehicle approached the front of the house.

"Not good," Anita said to herself. Both she and Xavier Perkins were trespassing. The small rundown house belonged to the estate of a rancher whose family had not yet decided what to do with it.

She didn't move or do anything for a minute or two. Xavier was a commercial truck driver who routinely stopped in Melrose on his travels. She had met him at the local truck stop over a year ago. Since then, one or two times each month, Anita would pick him up there, and they would go somewhere for the night. She liked Xavier. He was nice to her, and after their initial haggling over the price, he had never tried to jilt her.

The fact the she liked him was the main reason she didn't immediately drive off. Instead, after about five minutes, she crept back into the house to see what was happening.

She could hear the men arguing as soon as she entered the back bedroom. In addition to Xavier, she heard two other men's voices. They wanted something from him, but she couldn't tell what.

"How'd you get here?" One of the men asked.

"A friend dropped me off. The house is abandoned."

"We know it's not in your truck, so where is it?"

"Search the place. I don't have it. I've never seen it. I didn't take it."

The sound of a slap and then another startled Anita. She had half a mind to rush out there and defend her friend. She peeked around the door just as one of the men swung a machete, striking Xavier's arm as he raised it to defend himself. He screamed and collapsed to the floor.

Anita turned and ran back out the back door, oblivious to the noise she made. Her bad habit of leaving her keys in the ignition allowed her to start the Dodge and drive away before anyone could stop her. She knew a ranch trail ran from the back of the house she could use to get to a paved road. She also knew a place she could hide her van near the intersection of the dirt trail and the paved road. She could hide there until the men left. She didn't think much past that. In the morning, she would drive back and check on Xavier.

One of the men spotted the van as it drove off. He heard the noise Anita made in her rush to leave, and he reached the back door just as she drove away. The dark night and open terrain behind the house enabled him to follow the van's headlights. He didn't want to watch his partner's vicious interrogation tactics. He'd seen them many times before.

Watching the van gave him the opportunity to remain out back. He saw the lights of the van turn off at the same time Xavier's screams momentarily stopped. He wondered why the van didn't keep driving away. He smiled, shouted at his partner that he would be back, and started walking toward the van.

Chapter 2

Chubbs started barking at the door before the doorbell rang. I stepped out of my kitchen and saw a shadow through the front door's glazed side panel. The person rang the doorbell, and Chubbs immediately hid in the den, peering round the corner. I never considered him a guard dog.

I looked at my watch. I didn't get many visitors and fewer still at eight-thirty in the morning. At least I had put on a pair of jeans this morning to go with the ENMU tee shirt I had slept in. I opened the door.

"Mr. West, I need your help."

She looked a mess. I saw a dirt bike parked on the street. A blue helmet was fastened to the seat. She didn't look old enough to be driving it.

"Why?"

"Can I come in?"

"Why?" I asked again. I could've asked a more intelligent question, but my mind had started running in a bunch of different directions. The loudest thing running through my mind was a danger warning. Underage girls don't normally show up at my door asking to come in. Hell, grown-up women don't either.

"Please, my mother is missing, and I'm afraid they will be coming after me."

Chubbs hurried over to her. She bent down and petted him. Both Chubbs and the girl looked up at me with pleading eyes.

"I'm not a private investigator. You should go to the police."

"I have." She didn't say more. She didn't need to.

I studied her for a few seconds. She had short curly brown hair and despite the smudges of dirt on her face, she was quite pretty. I realized the tear in her jeans was likely intentional. Her black leather jacket had two dried mud spots on her left sleeve.

Chubbs had moved around and sat next to her, facing the door. I could've ignored them both. My brain was still flashing danger signs. This could be a setup. I had made enough enemies in the last decade. She could later claim I tried to sexually assault her.

The smell of burning bacon finally broke the impasse. "Come on in and have a seat. I need to turn off the stove."

I hurried to the kitchen and moved the frying pan off the stove. Chubbs came in and did his little happy dance.

"Traitor," I said.

Chapter 3

She stood in the middle of the room with her hands clasped in front of her. I thought I could see some trepidation in her eyes. Chubbs had moved back next to her side.

"Sit down, please. Want some coffee?"

"No, thank you," she said. She sat on the couch. Chubbs moved over to his large pillow on the floor.

I had my coffee in hand, so I sat on my recliner. "What's your name?"

"Jessica. I live near Melrose."

Melrose is a very small town a handful of miles west of Clovis. Near it meant in the middle of nowhere.

"Tell me in more detail why you're here."

"My aunt told me you can help people, and that I should ask you for help. She said you don't charge people. I don't have any money."

"That's not what I mean. What help are you looking for?"

"My mom is missing. I think she might be dead. Can you find her?" She said this without any obvious signs of emotion.

I wondered why there were no tears for her mom. "How long has she been missing?"

"Three weeks, today. It's not rare for her not to show up for a day or two, but never longer."

"No husband?"

"No. I never knew who my dad was."

Finally, a crocodile tear tried to escape her left eye. She looked away for a second.

"Any brothers or sisters?" I asked.

"No."

"You reported her missing to the Sheriff's office, right?"

"Yes. They did some checking and decided she had probably run off with some man. I don't think they are looking for her anymore."

"So, you came to me."

"Yes."

"Didn't your aunt tell you I wasn't a private investigator?"

"Yes, but she said that didn't matter."

"You said that whoever took her, if someone did, they might come for you now. Why do you think that?"

"Because someone, a man I believe, has been following me around."

"Have you reported this man to the police?"

"No. It's more of a feeling than anything else. I never saw someone, at least not enough of him to recognize him."

"But you're sure he's been following you?"

"Yes. I moved in with my aunt yesterday. It's just temporary. I'll probably go back home tomorrow."

"You came here from there?"

"No, I had to run out to the J Bar to take care of their horses. That's my job. I came here from there."

"You had to get up early."

"I always do. Will you help me?"

"You got a last name?"

"Perez, although I might change it."

"Getting married?"

She smiled. I thought she should do so more often. "No

chance."

"Your mom have the same last name?"

"Of course. Here's a picture of her. It's fairly recent. Her first name is Anita." She pulled a three by five-inch picture out of her jacket pocket.

I looked at it and could immediately see the resemblance with Jessica. "I'll need your phone number and address."

"What's your phone number?" she asked.

At first, I thought she was being cocky, but then I remembered I wasn't young anymore. People no longer write on paper. They prefer to do everything by phone. I gave her my number, and within seconds, she texted me the contact information I had requested.

"Okay, I'll ask around and do some checking. No promises. I drive a black Mustang, so if you see it out by your place, it's just me."

"Thank you, Mr. West." She stood up. "Are you going to talk to my aunt? Her name is Vicky. She's real nice."

"Yes."

She smiled again. "Good, I included her phone number, too. She'll be excited."

I followed her to the front door and watched her leave. I also wondered what I had just gotten myself into. How did I let these things happen? I rationalized that my involvement would be limited. Certainly, within a week, two at the max, I could extricate myself from any commitment she thinks I made to her. After all, what in the world could I do that the police haven't already done?

Her aunt's name, Vicky Perez, didn't ring any bells. I wondered how she knew to send Jessica to me. And why?

Chubbs looked up at me and appeared to be very pleased with himself.

"Give me a break," I said, and went to the kitchen to salvage my breakfast.

Chapter 4

My bacon did not appear salvageable, so I tossed it in the trash and decided to head out for donuts. I slipped on my crocs and a barely wrinkled long sleeve shirt. Late April usually had cool mornings and warm afternoons in this part of New Mexico. I left Chubbs curled up asleep on his pillow.

Usually, the thought of getting a couple cinnamon cake donuts would be enough to cheer me up. It didn't today. I was angry with myself. I had no business telling Jessica I would help her. I was also angry at her and her aunt. Why did they have to pick on me to help out? Money was the obvious answer. Real private investigators charge a fee.

"Are you okay?" Nancy asked.

I looked up. "Yes. Why do you ask?"

"You usually come in smiling and saying hello to all of us. Today you barely grumbled out your order, came right here, and have been staring at your donuts for the last minute or two. Normally, you would have wolfed them down by now." She had a point.

"It's been a bad morning."

"Want to talk about it?" She sat on the bench on the other side of the booth. "Women trouble?"

Nancy and I had become friends over the last several years. Our association had developed during my weekly visits to her donut shop. I figured she was my age, around fifty, but she could've been a few years older. I liked her and her husband.

"You know I lead a monk-like existence. I like it. Today, my dog made me do something I didn't want to do. You have a cat, right?"

"Yes."

"Want to trade?"

"Maybe. What did he make you do?"

"I had a young kid come to the house this morning and asked me to help her find her mother."

"I didn't think you did that kind of thing."

"I don't. That's the point."

"But your dog made you say you would," she said grinning. "Is she really missing?"

"I think so, but it's been a few weeks."

"So, you think she might not want to be found, or maybe she's being held against her will."

"Or worse. She may be dead," I said.

"Oh, poor girl. No dad, I guess."

I shook my head. "She's been to the police."

"They probably think she's run off with someone."

"They know all the possibilities, but they have nothing to go on and too many other priorities. It's not their fault."

"And you don't." I didn't answer right away. "What's her name? Can you tell me."

"Jessica Perez, she lives out by Melrose. Mom's name is Anita."

"I don't know her."

"Didn't think you would. How's Dale?"

"He's hanging in there." She sounded resigned. Dale, her husband, had prostate cancer that had metastasized.

"Tell him hello for me and to stay strong."

"I will, and Jim," she said and paused.

"Yes."

"I'm glad you're going to help this girl."

"You and my dog," I said.

She smiled and went back behind the counter.

I took my time eating the two donuts and sipping on my coffee. Before leaving, I purchased a dozen glazed. The drive to the Curry County Sheriff's Office only took a few minutes. I didn't think it was necessary, but a dozen donuts would always be appreciated.

Before entering, I called Deputy Johnny Willis. I had known him most my life, and while we weren't close, I thought he would be a good starting point. As I waited for someone to track him down, I wondered if I should have contacted him first before investing in the donuts.

"Hey, Jim, what can I do for you today?" Johnny asked when he made it to his phone.

"Do you have five minutes. I'm outside and would like to come in and talk to you. I have donuts."

"You said the magic words. I'll meet you out front." He must have been close, as he showed up within a few seconds.

We shook hands and said a few things that people usually say after not seeing each other in a while. I noticed he had a lot less hair than the last time I saw him. He took the donuts and escorted me inside. "Have you been here before?" he asked.

"A few times a few years ago," I said.

"Oh yeah, that guy who tried to kill you. Hope this isn't something similar."

"No, not at all. I was approached this morning by a young woman, a Jessica Perez, whose mother is missing. She also thinks she might be in danger, but has no explanation for either. She and her mom live out by Melrose. Are you familiar with it?"

"Not at all, but there is no reason why I should be. If the daughter reported it to us, I can hook you up with Mitch Amon. He heads up that branch."

"I'd appreciate it. She said she did report it."

"I didn't think you did this kind of stuff."

"I don't and don't want to. She just caught me at a weak moment."

"Getting soft?" he asked with a smile. When I didn't answer, he said he would take me to see Mitch. On the way, he dropped off the box of donuts next to the office coffee pot. Two deputies I didn't know immediately stood up and started walking toward the donuts.

We didn't have to walk far. Mitch was in a private office studying something on his computer. He looked up when Johnny tapped on his door.

"Mitch, you have a minute?"

"For you, I have two," Mitch said. He looked at me. I thought I saw some recognition in his face, but I didn't recall ever meeting him. He stood up. Tall and thin, he wore his jet-black hair a little longer than most of the men in the building.

"This is an old friend of mine, Jim West. He was approached by a young lady who asked him for some help. It deals with a matter you may be investigating," Johnny said.

"Please have a chair, Jim," Mitch said.

"I'll leave you two to discuss it. I have to get to a meeting," Johnny said and left.

"Thanks for seeing me, Mitch."

"You have ten minutes. I'm all ears."

I went through the details of that morning, leaving out Chubb's involvement. He said he was familiar with the case.

"What does she think you can do that we can't?"

"Good point, I even told her that."

"Are you a licensed private investigator? I didn't think you were."

"No, and I told her that." His comment told me that he knew a lot more about me than most people in town. "Is there anything you can tell me that I can use to tell her that you guys are on top of this?"

"I wish I could, Jim, but to be honest, we don't have the slightest idea where she could be. She has a history of disappearing for a day or two. No real steady job, and the ones she has the most experience with are not ones I'd want any women in my family to do. She's been arrested for soliciting a half dozen times, but not in the past few years."

"Do you think she's still alive?"

"Who knows? Without a body or some other hard evidence, we have to go with the likelihood she still is. We've taken all the usual steps and have come up with zilch. One interesting thing, though, no one we talked to was surprised she's disappeared, and no one seemed to care."

"That's kind of sad. The daughter cares," I said.

"Yes. I hope you can help her."

His comment surprised me. "I don't see how."

"Me neither, but she's had a rough life. You don't expect to get paid, do you?"

"No. I don't do this stuff, so why would I charge anyone. Life in near poverty is not such a bad thing."

He grinned, "Tell me about it. So, what are you going to do?"

"I was hoping you would tell me to stay out of it."

"Out of what? We have no leads to pursue. Sad thing is we're sitting here hoping the woman shows back up, too."

"You're depressing me."

"Listen, we have a rookie who still gets emotional over all these missing people. He also needs more street time. He hasn't yet learned how to carry on a conversation with a witness. These kids do everything by phone. Sit them across the table from someone, and they're lousy at interviewing." He shook his head. "Why don't I have him drive you out to their place, talk to the daughter again, and see some of the neighbors. It'll be good experience for him, and it will help you placate the daughter."

"You really want me to do this?"

"Sounds like you already got yourself into it."

He had a point.

"Besides, if I told my wife you came by today because you were trying to help a teenager find her missing mom, she'd kick me out of the house if I told you to stay out of it. She's kind of a fan."

"Do I know your wife, Mitch?"

"I doubt it, but a lot of people in town know you. It's not a big town."

"Tell her not to believe everything she sees on the internet."

Chapter 5

I called Vicky, who turned out to be a Perez, too. She reacted like she expected my call and insisted I come right over. I agreed, but a little piece of my mind kept telling me I needed to stop letting other people dictate what I do and when. I'd work on that later, I thought, as I drove to Vicky's address in extreme south Clovis.

She lived in a small neighborhood located next to the main road that runs from Clovis to Portales. Her house looked like all the other dozen or so on the street. They were likely built at the same time in the 1950's or 60's. Back then the nearby railroad kept hundreds of people employed.

I turned onto her short driveway and noticed a woman stood in the open doorway. She walked to my car as I climbed out. "Mr. West, is that you?" She smiled and held out her hand.

"That's me," I said and shook her hand.

"Oh, I'm so glad you are going to help my Jessie."

"I'm not sure there is much I can do."

"Please come in. I have some freshly baked cookies and coffee." She grabbed my wrist and tugged at me to follow.

Something about her struck me as curious. She wore nice slacks and a white blouse with ruffles at the end of the sleeves and a long neckline that showed ample cleavage. Her black hair had been combed, and she had put on enough makeup that even I noticed.

"Am I keeping you from something?"

"No, not at all, I'm free all morning," she said and smiled. "Please have a seat. I do need to talk to you about my sister."

She motioned to the couch, and I sat down. She disappeared into another room, returning moments later with a silver serving tray. A plate with at least a dozen cookies sat on it along with two empty cups, a silver coffee pot, a side bowl with sugar, and a miniature silver pitcher containing milk.

"Oh, Vicky, this is too much."

"Not at all," she said, smiling and sitting down next to me. She poured the coffee into a cup and handed it to me.

"I told your niece that I didn't think I could do much to help."

"Well, I personally think Nita has run off for good. She's talked about it in the past."

"Why would she do that?"

"Like I said, she has always dreamt about visiting Europe."

She hadn't said that, at least to me, but I kept the thought to myself. "Would she abandon her daughter without saying anything?"

"Jessie's a grown up. She's seventeen or eighteen. She's sweet, and I love her, but she doesn't need her mom around. You know, Nita is my sister, but she wasn't a very good mom. The Richardsons have done more to take care of Jessie than her mom ever did."

"The Richardsons?" I asked.

"They own the J Bar ranch and have had Jessie take care of their horses since she was twelve. They pay her and treat her like one of their own."

"What can you tell me about your sister?"

"First, have a cookie." She put two on a napkin and handed them to me.

"Thanks, chocolate chip is one of my favorites."

"Nita has been a disappointment. She's been arrested a number of times, but I guess the police can tell you about that. She drinks too much, smokes too much, and isn't picky about the men she spends time with. There's not much she wouldn't do for a few bucks."

"That's too bad."

"My point is that if she ran into some old geezer with money, she'd take off with him anywhere for as long as the money lasted."

"Does she have a passport?"

"I doubt it."

"Have you heard from her in the past couple of weeks."

"No, but she rarely called me unless she was drunk, or wanted money, or was in jail."

"Was that often?"

"Not so much the past year or two," she said.

"How would you recommend I go about tracing her whereabouts?"

"I have no idea. I guess she could be dead. I mean she could've gotten into the wrong car. You understand?"

I did. "Was that something she would do?"

"It may not sound like it, but I love my sister. Somewhere in her teen years, she discovered she could make more money with her body than I could ever make flipping burgers at Foxy's Drive In. She never finished high school. Somehow, she found a man who married her when she was twenty. That's how she got that house of theirs. They weren't married two years when he was struck by lightning of all things."

"Was he Jessie's father?"

"Good heavens, no. She wasn't born until eight or nine years later. Nita had herself fixed when Jessie was born, so she wouldn't have any more kids."

We talked for another ten minutes before I made my escape. The image of Anita Perez was not one I liked. I wondered if Jessie wasn't better off with her mother gone. During the ten-minute drive back to my house, I considered the possibility that Anita was dead. That made more sense to me. Any person might want to run off and escape their situation, but it was hard for me to believe she wouldn't make some contact with her child or sister at some point after her departure.

I tried to reach back into my memory to find a missing person case where there was a family left behind, and no one heard from the missing person. I could think of a few teenagers who ran away from a bad home environment, but I couldn't remember a single mother abandoning a child, or teenager, without making some sort of contact a few days or weeks later.

My phone came alive as I pulled into my garage. The first text came from Jessica, thanking me for talking to her aunt. The second came from Mitch, advising me that a Deputy Josh Dillard would be contacting me about the missing person matter. The third came as an actual call once I stepped out of my car.

"Mr. West, I'm Deputy Dillard with the Curry County Sheriff's Office. My boss asked me to call you."

"I just received a text from him."

"He wants me to take you out to the Perez place. Are you free tomorrow morning?"

"Yes, what time would you like to go?"

"I'll pick you up at nine if that's okay."

I agreed, and he ended the call. The way Dillard said Mitch

wanted him to take me out to the Perez place piqued my curiosity. I would have thought he would say his boss wanted him to go out there to ask a few more questions, and that I should ride along. I didn't mind being chauffeured around, but that's not how it usually worked.

I decided to mow my yard. The grass had only started growing again, but the weeds were in full takeover mode. The day had already turned warm and there wasn't a cloud in sight.

Chapter 6

He stood inside Jessie's back door. She had left it unlocked. Good luck for him, he thought. The last two times he came by here, all the doors were locked. He knew she wouldn't be returning home any time soon, and he was content with that. He could always come back while she was here.

He found her bedroom and stood by her bed for a while. He imagined what it would be like being alone with her. Moving over to her closet, he opened it and felt a blue blouse that hung in the middle of several other blouses. The blue looked like the color of his mother's eyes, and that made him smile.

The room darkened as the sun went behind a cloud. He hurried out of the room to the living room where a large window allowed more daylight to come into the room. Nothing moved in the front yard. He saw his car and wondered if he should've parked it somewhere else. As he stood there, the small cloud moved past the sun, and the world, inside and out, brightened.

He returned to the bedroom determined to find something he could take with him. It didn't take long. He found an item in the second drawer he opened. Folding them, he placed them in his jeans pocket. He would leave them in his pocket until he was back in his room alone. Later, he could always return them to her. The thought made him smile.

In the kitchen, he found a soft drink in the refrigerator and sat down at the small kitchen table to drink it. He would like to own a house like this and wondered how many acres of property it had. One could never tell by looking. The nearest neighbors were a mile or so away. He knew that, but looking out back, the land seemed to go on forever without another home or building in sight. The back yard could be one acre or fifty acres. Without a fence, and there wasn't one, who could tell.

He jumped up when he heard an airplane roar overhead. A second one followed it. He looked out the kitchen door and saw two air force jets flying off in the distance. He had seen them before but only a couple of times.

Returning to the table, he considered looking for something to eat but decided he didn't want Jessie to know someone had been inside her house. He may want to come back later, and he didn't need her to start locking the doors.

He sat there and let his imagination roam. Maybe he wanted to stay there until she came home. She might be happy to see him. As far as he knew, she didn't have a boyfriend. He looked at his watch.

"Damn," he muttered to himself. He was going to be late.

He left the house the same way he came in and drove away, thinking he could always come back.

Chapter 7

D eputy Dillard parked on the street in front of my house at two minutes before nine. The county sedan looked shiny and new in the morning sun. From my dining room window, I watched him step out of the car before I left the house.

"Deputy Dillard?" I asked, although I knew it had to be him.

"Yes, sir, but please call me Josh."

We shook hands on my sidewalk. I fought the urge to ask him why he wasn't in school. He didn't look over twenty. He was nearly my height at six foot and thin. Lanky is the word that came to mind.

"I'm ready to go, if you are," I said.

"Yes, sir. I have an extra cup of coffee from Starbucks for you in the car. If you don't want it, Mr. West, that's no problem."

"Sounds good, thanks, and please, call me Jim." I noticed his shoes were shined and his uniform had been pressed recently. The inside of the Sheriff's vehicle looked like it had just been detailed.

"Yes, sir. Oh, excuse me," he grinned. "I called Ms. Perez, so she knows we're coming out there. Have you met her?"

"I have."

"It's terrible that her mom is missing," Josh said. He stopped at the intersection next to my house and waited for an SUV to go by. He had the time to go, but I guessed he wanted to be extra careful with me in the car.

"Yes, it is. Unfortunately, I doubt if there's much we can do for her."

"Think she's still alive?"

"Fifty-fifty, but I have a bad feeling."

"Me, too," Josh said. "The fact that she hasn't contacted anyone, and there is no evidence she has used her one credit card, makes me think she may be dead."

We left the city limits on Highway 60, driving past Cannon AFB. Josh maintained a constant speed two miles an hour under the posted speed limit. I wondered if he was doing it for me, or if he was always a slow driver. Cars and trucks of all types shot by us, despite the vehicle we were in.

"How long have you been with the Sheriff's department?"

"Nearly six months."

I sensed pride in his voice. We talked a little about working in law enforcement and then about the new restaurant from a national chain opening in Clovis. In a town the size of Clovis, a new restaurant can be big news.

About a mile before we reached the small town of Melrose, Josh turned off the highway onto a narrow county road. He didn't seem to be using any navigation help.

"You've been out here before," I said.

"No, but I studied the route last night on my laptop. I think I have it memorized. What's she like?"

"Jessica?"

"Yes. I mean is she going to get all emotional on us? Or angry?"

"Don't overthink this. She's a sharp kid and has been through a lot." I imagined Josh was going through all types of scenarios in his mind.

When we pulled into the dirt driveway, the house and yard weren't what I expected. The house was old and small, but the yard around the house was well-maintained, and the house didn't have that run-down, neglected look. Jessie sat in a wooden chair on the small porch but stood as we came to a stop.

"Is that her?" he asked.

"Yes."

"Mr. West, I didn't know you were coming out, too." Jessie said as she approached us. She smiled at me before turning her attention to Josh.

"Jessie, this is Deputy Josh Dillard," I said as a way of introduction.

She looked at Josh, and I saw a hint of a smile. "Come inside, let's get out of this sun."

Once inside, Jessie directed us to a room to the right of the front door. The hardwood flooring looked old and scratched but had been swept clean. A baby blue sheet covered the small sofa. She had tucked in the sheet to make it look almost form-fitting. Two old chairs that looked like they may have come from a dining room table sat opposite the couch. A lamp sat on a small wooden end table positioned between the chairs. The couch faced a large front window that allowed plenty of daylight to enter the room.

"Can I get either of you some ice water?"

We both declined.

"Jessie," Josh said and then hesitated for a moment. "Can I call you Jessie?"

"Of course," she said.

"I've been tasked to take a more in-depth look into your mother's disappearance. Hopefully, we can develop something new. I'll do my best."

She looked at me.

"Deputy Dillard is familiar with the investigation but was not involved with it. He can bring some new ideas and may catch something the initial investigation missed."

"The Sheriff doesn't want this matter to become cold. If you don't mind, I need to ask you a few questions I'm sure you've already answered more than once," Josh said.

"I don't mind," Jessie said.

I thought Josh did a good job with the interview. He even let her talk when she got off on side topics. I'm not sure what new he may have discovered that wasn't already in the case file, but I learned that her mother had stopped bringing men to the house about four years earlier. She had no idea where her mother may have spent the nights when she was away.

"My mom is who she is. I'm not her, but I know she loves me. That's why none of this makes sense."

I felt like telling her there was one possibility that explained why she hadn't contacted her daughter, but thought better of it. Apparently, Josh did too. We were close to finishing the interview when Josh's phone chirped.

He answered it, looked at me for a minute, before saying he had to take the call outside. He hurried outside.

"Thanks for helping me, Mr. West," Jessie said.

"Jim."

"Jim," she smiled. "Even if you only could get the one deputy who's younger than me."

"He's older than you. A little," I said and grinned. "He seems sharp, too. By the way, I thought you were staying at your aunt's."

"I have, mostly, but I think I'll come back here now."

Josh poked his head back inside the door. "Mr. West, we need to go. Jessie, sorry, I'll call you later today and schedule a time to finish our conversation."

I could tell by Josh's voice something in the phone call had shaken him. I could tell Jessie sensed it, too.

"Is it about my mom?"

"I don't think so. It sounded like a traffic accident," Josh said. He turned and walked to the car before she could ask anything more.

"I'll let you know," I said to Jessie. She grabbed my wrist and then let go.

"Okay." She stood there and watched us go. I knew our sudden departure made her nervous.

By the time I got in the car, Josh already had a location displayed on the car's navigation system. He drove out of the driveway a little faster than I expected.

"A body has been found. My boss thinks it's her mom. He called us since we are already here. Others are on their way. He told me to bring you. I hope you don't mind."

I did, but I kept that to myself. "How far?"

"Not five minutes from here." He turned off the narrow road we were on onto another paved road barely wide enough for two cars. He accelerated to sixty miles an hour and turned on the car's flashers.

I felt like telling him to slow down, but I could see the road went straight and the terrain flat for as far as I could see.

Chapter 8

Josh started slowing down as soon as he saw the white pickup truck in the distance. "He's going to take us to the body."

I saw a rare clump of trees ahead to my right and a house up a very slight incline nearly a mile away. Nothing else appeared to be anywhere around us. A variety of low growing, wild plants dotted the landscape. Josh slowed the car to a crawl the last twenty yards. I wondered if he was being overly cautious or dreaded what he knew was coming.

A man dressed in jeans and a clean, white tee shirt stepped out of the truck and stood still, waiting for us. Josh stopped us about ten yards in front of him, and we both got out and approached him. The man appeared to be in his late sixties or early seventies.

"Mr. Reynolds?" Josh asked and extended his hand.

"Yes," the man said and reached for Josh's hand.

"I'm Deputy Josh Dillard and this is Mr. Jim West."

The man didn't look at me. "She's in the van by the trees. I don't want to go back over there."

"We'll need you to show us --."

"No." The man interrupted Josh. "It's right there. Take the dirt trail right behind my truck. It goes all the way to the house, but take a left just before you get to the trees. Right there, you can't get lost."

The trees were only thirty to forty yards away from the road.

"Mr. Reynolds," Josh started to speak, but the old man again cut him off.

"No."

"Will you stay here in your car until we find her, and one of us comes back to let you go?" I asked. "You say she's just there," I motioned at the trees, "but I can't see anything."

"There's a small culvert on the left side of the trees. She's in the van."

"Does the property belong to the house?" I asked, pointing to the house.

"Used to, but no one has lived in that house for a couple years."

"Will you stay?"

"Yes."

I turned to Josh, "Let's go check it out."

He didn't say anything until we were back in the car. "I think we should've forced him to come with us."

"That would've caused more problems than either of us need."

We drove by the pickup and saw the dirt trail that years earlier might have been considered a dirt road. Josh maneuvered the sedan to the patch of trees and turned left onto an even rougher looking trail.

"Stop here, Josh. I see the van."

We stopped, and both of us stared through the dozen or so trees and bushes at the top half of an old van.

"We need to be careful about messing up the crime scene."

"I know. I've worked crime scenes before." He sounded irritated.

"Sorry, I know this is your crime scene now," I said, telling myself as much as him that he needed to take charge.

We both stepped out of the car and followed the trail on foot as it led us around the edge of the trees and back into an open space where the van was parked. The front of the van faced us. A light coating of dust and sand covered the van. It looked like it hadn't been moved for a while. We stopped and studied the scene.

"The tailgate is open. I think she's back there," I said. The swarm of flying insects reinforced my guess.

"Stay here," Josh instructed and took some hesitant steps toward the driver's side of the van. He paused near the front driver's side door and peered through the window. He continued his slow walk and stopped. Suddenly, he took a quick step backwards and almost fell.

I had to give him credit. He put his hand in front of his mouth and nose and took a few more steps. When he reached a spot where he could see clearly into the back of the van, he stood still and stared at what was inside. A few seconds later, he turned and dashed to the nearest tree. Leaning against it, Josh threw up whatever breakfast he may have had.

I gave him a moment before I followed his tracks to the back of the van. One glance was all I needed. The body was that of a woman, but beyond that, the experts would have to identify her. Nature's scavengers and the daytime heat had left her unrecognizable. I knew better than to let my eyes linger on her. I didn't want to be hugging my own tree. Instead, I copied down the van's license tag number.

"Josh, let's get back to the man. Nothing we can do here."

He looked at me but didn't say anything. His face looked pale, and I thought that his eyes were a little out of focus. He started to wipe his face with his sleeve and paused. Grabbing a handkerchief out of a back pocket, he wiped his face.

"Come on. You'll feel better the further away from here we get."

Josh let go of the tree and took a couple unsteady steps toward me. I turned and started the trek back to the sedan. I didn't look back.

"Sorry about that," Josh said as he approached the car. We both got into the car before I said anything.

"No need to be sorry. Your reaction was typical of all of us. The first few times we see something like that, it happens."

"Do you get used to it?"

"No, but you learn to not look at them very long. Don't need to. Verify the person is dead, and let the experts tell you how they died. Look around the scene. That's where and how you contribute."

Josh drove us back onto the road next to where Reynolds was waiting. After he parked, Josh looked like he didn't want to get out of the car.

"I texted you the van's license number. Why don't you call it in along with confirming there is a body out here. I'll go talk to him," I said, motioning out the window with my head.

"Thanks."

"Mr. Reynolds, how did you happen to see the van? It's pretty well hidden." I asked. I leaned against his truck alongside him.

"About fifty yards down the road, back the way I came, you get a pretty good look at it for a few seconds. I saw it a few days ago but didn't think anything of it. I don't use this road very often. This morning it caught my eye. Well, the big black birds got my attention. I knew something wasn't right."

"So, you checked it out?"

"Wish I didn't. I can't get that sight out of my mind. I chased the birds away. Is she that missing woman?"

"You know about her?"

"Everyone here does," he said. "Can I go?"

"In a minute, the deputy is talking to his boss. More people are coming. I can't make that decision."

He looked at me like he wanted to ask, "Then what in the hell are you doing here?" It would've been a good question.

Josh walked over to us. "Mr. Reynolds, did you touch anything over there, like the van or something inside?"

"No way."

"That's good," Josh said. "You didn't pick up anything off the ground?"

"No. I saw her and got out of there as fast as I could."

"Do you mind letting me look at your driver's license?"

Reynolds looked at me. "We need to verify you are who you say you are, that's all," I said.

"That's right, Mr. Reynolds, then we can let you go on your way."

Reynolds handed him his license. Josh walked to the back of the pickup truck and took a photo of vehicle's license tag and Reynold's driver's license.

"I'm sorry for all this hassle. With all the scrutiny on the police these days, they have to be super thorough," I said. I moved slightly to my right to block Reynold's view of what Josh was doing. I didn't want him to get anymore agitated than he already was.

Josh returned the driver's license. "Mr. Reynolds, we can't be sure if the person in that van is the missing woman, but do you have any idea why she might have gone missing? "

"No, only gossip that I tend to ignore."

"And that being?" Josh asked.

"I'd rather not say, but you should talk to Chester Cobb. He seems to be the expert on her."

"How do we find him?"

"Well Deputy, it shouldn't be hard, he owns the truck stop on the highway. Can I go now?"

"Yes. Thank you very much for calling this in," Josh said.

Reynolds grumbled something to himself and walked to his truck. He drove off without a wave goodbye.

Chapter 9

Reynold's pickup hadn't gone a half mile down the road when I spotted the flashing lights of an approaching vehicle.

"Here come the reinforcements," Josh said.

Thirty minutes later, a dozen law enforcement officers along with the medical examiner and his assistant worked the crime scene. I stayed by Josh's car, out of the way and, for the most part, by myself. Finally, Josh joined me by the car.

"They want me to drive up to the house and verify no one is there. We know it's been vacant, but there might be squatters. After that, we can head back to Clovis."

"Okay. Let's do it," I said.

The condition of the dirt road kept our speed down. "I feel like I should call Jessie, but the boss said not to."

"Your boss probably doesn't want her jumping into a car and racing out here. She doesn't need to see that."

"Oh, yeah. I didn't think about that. You think anyone will be here?" he asked as we pulled to a stop behind the house.

"Doesn't look like it," I said. I didn't see evidence of anything being taken care of or disturbed in the back yard or the back of the house.

We both got out of the car. Josh peered through a back window while I knocked on the back door.

"I can't see anyone. There's still furniture in there." He walked over to me, and I knocked again. "Should we try the door?"

"Might as well," I said.

"It's not locked," Josh said, pushing the door open. "Hello, anyone there? We're the police." Josh took one step inside and froze. He spun around, wide-eyed, and covered his nose and mouth with his hand. He hurried outside. "Something stinks."

Despite my distance from the door a faint odor reached me. I immediately thought I knew what caused it. "You need to go back inside and check it out. Don't touch anything. You may have another crime scene."

"Shouldn't I call them to send someone else up here?"

"You can, but everyone is going to ask why you couldn't or wouldn't check it out. Do you want that?"

He looked down at the ground and shook his head.

"Hold a handkerchief against your mouth and nose, or if you have a Covid mask in your vehicle, get that and put it on."

"Good idea," he said and retrieved a mask from the car. After positioning it on his face, he asked me if I wanted to go in with him.

"No, this is your scene and keeping me out is a good first step in preserving it."

He nodded, turned, and ventured back inside. Less than a minute later, he came out, ripping the mask off his face. I thought he might be sick again, but this time, he pulled his phone out of his pocket and called his boss.

"We've got another body," he said. "Yes, up here in the house. A man, I think." He listened for a short while. "Yes, I will." The call ended.

Josh turned to face me. "He looked really bad. Someone cut him up real bad."

"What did your boss tell you?"

"To secure the scene. I'm not sure what the scene is. You think the whole house?"

"It's a good choice. Let's walk around the house and tape off any entry area. We can also do a first look for anything of interest."

After retrieving a roll of crime scene tape from the trunk of the car, Josh closed the back door of the house and used the tape to make a large X, sealing off the entrance. We walked around the house and observed nothing of interest. The windows all appeared to be locked or stuck shut. The front door was closed. Josh didn't see if it was locked. Rather, he placed the crime scene tape across it.

"I don't want to disturb any possible fingerprints," he said.

"Good thinking. How long do you think the man inside has been dead?"

"I have no idea. A while though, there were maggots," he stopped talking.

"I was just wondering if he might have been killed the same time as the woman in the van. Not the same moment, but both killed within a few hours of each other."

"You think that's what happened?"

"I don't know, Josh. It's a theory that makes more sense to me than two people killed on this land at roughly the same time and not being connected."

"You should mention it to them when they get here. I bet you're right."

We had walked around the house and were in the backyard when a sheriff's vehicle with its flashers on slowly approached the house. "I suggest you mention it to them. I don't need any credit for anything."

"It's the sheriff," he said when the car came to a stop in front of us. I sensed a little apprehension in his voice.

The passenger window went down. An arm came out of the window and motioned for Josh to approach.

"We better go see what he wants," Josh said.

"No, you go, remember this is your scene. Don't keep him waiting."

Josh trotted the fifteen yards to the car. He leaned close to the window. Neither spoke loud enough for me to hear anything. Twice during the conversation Josh looked at me before turning his attention back to the sheriff. When the vehicle the sheriff was in backed away, did a U-turn, and began driving back toward the original crime scene, I walked over to Josh.

"Everything okay?" I asked.

"Yes. Thanks for the help today."

"I didn't do anything."

"Actually, you did. He asked me if I kept you out of the house. I said yes, but you know you made me go in there by myself."

"It's how we all learn."

"This, no, these were the first two homicides where I was the first responder. I don't think I screwed up anything."

"A perfect record," I said.

He laughed. "My reward is that I get to stay here all day guarding this house. The medical examiner will be up in a few minutes, but by the time the forensics team gets done down there and then up here, it will be dark."

"Should I be calling a cab?"

"No, the sheriff said he'll be sending someone up here to take you home. He also said that we shouldn't contact Jessie about this until they've removed both bodies. He said I could probably call her tonight."

"I'm surprised she hasn't tried to contact me," I said.

"If she does, please don't tell her anything. The sheriff said he didn't want you to be talking to anyone about this."

"I won't."

"I know. I told him I didn't think you would. What do you think happened here? Why weren't they both killed here if it was related?"

"Good question. There could be a few reasonable explanations, but I'll let you come up with those. I'm just a guest."

We both leaned against the side of the car, and Josh came up with three plausible theories for the answer to his own question.

Chapter 10

I received a text from Jessie while I was being driven home by a deputy I hadn't met before. Jessie wanted to know if we were coming back, and if our departure had anything to do with her mother. I sent her a text back saying they kept me away from the scene, but I was sure Deputy Dillard would be contacting her soon to answer her questions.

The deputy tasked with driving me home had obviously not been at either crime scene or been briefed in any detail on what had been found. "Two bodies, hell, that's a big deal for Melrose. Probably another murder suicide, we get those now and then," he said.

He might have been trying to get me to fill him in with what happened, but for several reasons, I didn't go there.

"I think two bodies would be a big deal for most places," I said.

"Except for big cities. Too much gang violence nowadays."

"That's true."

"Do you listen to the Albuquerque news?"

"I try not to," I said.

He started telling me about the gangs in Albuquerque and then went on to the Mexican cartels. The world was going to hell, he said more than once. I tended to agree with him.

A few hours after he dropped me off at my house, Josh called. "It's her, Jessie's mom. The van is registered to her, and they found her purse undisturbed under the driver's seat. It had her license in it. They think they know who the man is too, but his wallet was missing. He's a truck driver. He's also been missing for a while."

"Should you be telling me all this?"

"Yes, my boss said to fill you in. He said you were there."

"Are you going to tell Jessie?"

"Yes. I'm waiting for another deputy who specializes in this. She and I will go out to Jessie's house as soon as she gets here. I'm not looking forward to it," Josh said.

"Jessie sent me a text a little while ago wanting to know what was going on. I claimed ignorance but said you would get in touch with her later today. She didn't text me back."

"Thanks, Mr. West."

We ended the call. I had already made up my mind that the dead woman was Jessie's mother. I hoped that Jessie didn't insist on seeing her right away. I only took a glance at her, but I wouldn't want that vision to haunt her daughter for the rest of her life.

For the next twenty-four hours, I kept myself busy trying to patch the cinder block wall that served as a fence around my backyard. Over the years, cracks had formed in the grout, and part of the wall had separated. It still stood upright, but a good bump would likely knock it over. I had had a work crew look at it. They quoted me an astronomical figure to fix it.

I decided to fix it myself, but after weeks of half-hearted attempts, I hadn't gotten far. When my phone rang, I took the interruption as a sign that I had worked long enough.

"Mr. West, can I come talk to you again?"

"Sure, Jessie. I'm sorry about your mother."

"Are you home now?"

"Yes, but I've been working on my fence. I'm dirty and sweaty."

"That's okay. I'll be there in about five minutes." I heard her motorcycle engine revving right before the call ended.

I left all my tools and supplies in the yard and went inside to change shirts and wash my face and hands. I was still in the bathroom when my doorbell rang.

"Thanks for seeing me, Mr. West," she said when I let her in.

She wore blue jeans, black boots, and a navy-blue tee shirt under a light weight, black jacket. I figured that was her go-to motorcycle outfit.

"Please, call me Jim."

She sat down on my couch, and I sat in a nearby chair.

"My aunt said I should come by and thank you for, in her words, 'lighting a fire under the cops'."

"I really didn't do anything."

"Of course you did. Josh even said you were a giant help."

"Are you doing okay?" I wanted to get her off the delusion that I somehow helped in the discovery of her mom.

"Yes. I guess I knew something had happened to her. She wasn't the best mom, but I knew if she could, she would've contacted me. I think deep down, I always knew she wasn't alive."

"Still, I'm very sorry."

She nodded, but I could sense she had something else on her mind. "Do they think she was with the other man who was killed."

"Probably, but that's only a guess."

"She liked this one."

"You knew him?"

"No. Most the time, when she would get dressed up to go out, she had this look. It's hard to explain, but it's like she was going to a job she wished she didn't have to do."

I wondered if Jessie believed this to help convince herself that her mom felt like she had no choice.

"I tried to tell her a hundred times that she didn't need to go out, but she always did. Every now and then, she got into a routine with one man she liked. She was different then. She was like she was going out on a date. Happy, humming to herself," she said.

"And she was like this that night?"

"Yes. I've thought about it a lot. For the past six months or so, maybe longer, it seemed like there were one or two nights a month that she was like that. I had the feeling it was the same man. She was very relaxed."

"Do you know where they found her?"

"Yes. Josh told me everything."

"Would she have been familiar with that house?"

"Yes."

I thought she wanted to say more but didn't.

"Do you have someone to talk to about all this?"

"You mean besides you?"

"Yes, someone like your aunt."

"Yes, I spent the night at her house last night. We stayed awake way after midnight talking and crying."

"Good."

"And Josh," she added. "I can talk to him."

"I wish I could've done more for you and the ending was better."

"I do have one thing I'm worried about. Not all that long ago, but after she went missing, when I returned home from work, I noticed that someone had been in my house. A few things had been moved around, and a couple cokes were missing from the fridge. Nothing else was missing."

"Could that have been your mom?"

"I didn't think so. She doesn't drink cokes. Only I do, and an unopen pack of cigarettes was still on the kitchen counter. She would've taken those. I thought it was just some teenagers, but I've kept the house locked from then on. Now I wonder if someone came to the house looking for something else."

She had a good point.

"Did you tell the police?"

"Yes. Not at first, but I did later when I thought someone might be following me. I mentioned it to Josh yesterday."

"Good. There might be a connection. Do you feel safe there?"

"At home? Yes, although I might get a dog now. My mom didn't like pets. She said we couldn't afford them."

"Are you going to stay at your house?"

"Yes. The house is paid off. I can't afford to go anywhere else. Besides I like it there, and I can't imagine not working for the Richardsons. They need me, and I love their horses."

I didn't think taking care of a couple of horses would be much of a career, but I kept my thoughts to myself. I had already decided she had a rough future ahead of her.

"Jim, I need you to teach me how to shoot a gun, a pistol." The request came out of the blue and surprised me.

"Why would you need me to do that?"

"Josh suggested I get one and learn how to use it. He said because of his job he can't teach me, but once I learned we could practice together. Later, he said he shouldn't have even recommended I get one. I guess because of my age and his job."

"How old are you?"

"Just about nineteen, I'm old enough."

Old enough to make a lot of mistakes, I thought.

"Have you ever fired a weapon before?"

"I had a boyfriend who took me out on his parent's ranch to shoot jackrabbits with his rifle. I never hit one. I didn't want to, but they are pests."

"Do you have a current boyfriend?"

"Not since high school. I don't think I need or want one right now. Why? Do you date younger women?" I knew she was just teasing me.

I shook my head and grinned. "I can't keep up with them anymore."

She laughed. "Why are you interested?"

"No good reason, I was curious if you had anyone out there close you could call for help. It's my male chauvinism, thinking you need a man to protect you."

"That's why I want a dog, and why I want to learn how to shoot. Josh walked through my house and recommended additional locks and a security system."

"Can you afford all that?"

"Josh said he could front me the money for the security system, and I could pay him back over time. It's not that expensive. I haven't solved the gun issue. He said he couldn't pay for that."

"You like Josh?"

She blushed for a second. "He's nice, but he's only doing his job, and besides, I don't need a boyfriend right now."

"None of my business anyway."

She didn't say anything for a second. Her face hardened. "He recommended I don't try to see my mom right away."

"Do you understand why?"

She nodded her head.

"Will you teach me how to shoot, Jim?"

"Yes." I'm not sure how that word got out of my mouth. My mind kept telling me not to get involved.

Chapter 11

I had second thoughts as I drove down Mickie's driveway. The asphalt driveway needed resurfacing, but the weeds that tried to grow through the cracks had all been trimmed down. The new addition to the old house looked out of place, but I knew Mickie didn't care. She planned on living here until she died, and had told me more than once her kids could worry about selling it. When I asked her about her kids, she always changed the subject.

Mickie had served a number of years in the U.S. Army with multiple deployments to Iraq and Afghanistan. To describe her as 'tough as nails' would be an understatement. I had met her a few years earlier after an old acquaintance sent me an email suggesting I do so. He had said that the way I was going, she might be able to help me add a few years to my life. I knew he was referring to my surviving a recent attempt on my life.

I surprised myself by taking him up on his advice and reached out to Mickie. Despite her almost perfected, anti-social façade, we had hit it off about as well as expected.

When I turned off my car's engine, Mickie's two large boxers started circling the car and snarling. They intimidated me, and Mickie knew it. In the past, I had seen her more than once watching out the window to see what I would do. I had called her, so I knew it was only a matter of time before she would step outside and call the two Cujos off.

I watched as she stepped outside and smiled at me. I told myself her smile meant she was pleased to see me, but deep down I wondered if she was thinking how much fun it would be to turn her dogs loose on me.

She shouted something that I couldn't hear over the dogs barking. The dogs heard her and ran over to her. I stepped out of the car. "Mickie, thanks for seeing me today."

"Always good to see my favorite bachelor. Come on in."

Rather than wait for me, she walked toward me while I approached her. It still amazed me that when she wore long pants, it was almost impossible to tell that she had left nearly half of her left leg in Afghanistan. The missing little finger in her left hand was more obvious.

She kept her greying hair short and didn't seem to have any interest in dyeing it or even combing it. I imagined she was probably prettier than she first appeared, but she had little interest in doing anything to prove it. On the other hand, she had kept herself in shape. Somewhere in the house she likely had a work out area. All five foot six or seven of her looked like she did daily workouts of some type.

I walked with her into her house. Unlike most homes, the front door took you directly into a room that she had turned into her office, a very cluttered office. Mickie had everything one might need to repair and possibly manufacture all types of weapons. She kept the equipment she needed for routine maintenance and care here. The heavier equipment she kept in her barn.

"Staying busy?" I asked.

"Too much so." She looked around for a second, "Let's sit over there." She led me to a corner of the room where two chairs had ended up. She turned the one chair that was pressed against the wall around, so it would face outward, and slid the second chair away to make some space for us to sit down.

"Now explain to me again what's going on."

I told her everything I could remember about my encounters with Jessie and what had happened to her mother. I didn't intend to, but every time I thought I had said enough, Mickie would simply say, "And, what else."

"She wants to learn how to shoot." I finally said when I couldn't think of any more background.

"Smart girl. How old is she?"

"She says she'll be nineteen soon. I don't know when soon is."

"Okay, and you want to bring her here to teach her."

"Yes, and no. You would be the better teacher."

"That's obvious. I've seen you shoot," she said without grinning.

"Would you? I would pay for the lessons. She doesn't have any money."

"I would do it for free."

Her comment surprised me. She had once told me how much she would charge me for lessons. The price was ridiculously high. I decided to use her firing range but practice on my own.

"Thanks. She can use my Beretta, and I'll supply the ammo," I said.

"Do they know who killed her mom?"

"Not yet."

"And you said someone might be watching her."

"Yes, but that may be her imagination."

"Probably is. Bring her by, and we'll see how it goes. Do you want to practice some today? The range is clear."

"For a little while," I said.

Mickie's firing range wasn't your normal firing range. The

NRA would've scoffed at it, and the regulators would never let it open. One had to know Mickie to use it. She didn't advertise or accept payment for its use. She charged for her time, if one wanted lessons, and like I mentioned, she wasn't cheap.

I went out back by myself. I had been there enough times to know the routine. About fifty yards behind the house, the ground sloped downward to an extremely wide, dry creek bed. Once down the slope, the terrain leveled off, and a couple benches marked the beginning of the firing range. Nothing else did. For three hundred yards, the ground remained flat. Mickie told me that eons of rare but violent flooding carved this stretch. The far bank that climbed some ten to twelve feet served as a good backstop. Some rounds may have found their way over this natural barrier, but Mickie explained one had to travel for ten miles before hitting the next home.

Targets were the responsibility of the shooter. She didn't supply them, but a single post lay on the ground next to a post hole at fifty, seventy-five, one hundred, two hundred, and three hundred yards down the range. Users of the range had to put the posts in the post holes and attach their own targets. An old bicycle with big all terrain tires lay off to the side. A shooter could use the bike to get to and from some of the longer-range targets.

A wooden bench and a metal trash can sat off to the side about ten yards down range. I routinely used these. One could move the bench closer or further, but I didn't. This was old fashioned target shooting. I took the empty coke and assorted beer cans out of the trash can and positioned them on the bench.

Shooting at a paper target served a purpose, but hitting a beer can and having it fly off the bench provided a more enjoyable type of feedback. I had become quite good at it over the past year.

I practiced different firing positions: standing, kneeling, squatting, and even walking. By the time I had used up my box of bullets, I was sweating. I picked up my expended shell casings and put all the soda and beer cans back into the trash can.

Mickie sat on her back porch and watched me return. "How'd you do?"

"Pretty good, I hit more cans than I missed."

She laughed. "You're lucky the cans don't shoot back. Listen, bring that girl here sooner rather than later."

"I will."

She walked me to my car. Her two dogs followed us.

"Tell your husband hello for me," I said.

She nodded, and I got in my car and drove off. For some odd reason, I always felt a little safer when I reached the main road, leaving her property behind. From what I understood, Mickie rarely left her property. Her husband spent most of the year abroad as part of the Doctors Without Borders program or something like it. I had never met him. In my always suspicious mind, I wondered if he even existed.

Although she never talked about her injury, a little snooping on the internet disclosed that she was part of a recon patrol that had run into serious trouble in the mountains in Afghanistan. She had to be rescued by helicopter. Only two soldiers from her team made it out alive, and Mickie had almost died from her injuries. Rumor had it the doctor who saved her later became her husband.

I assumed the military had medically retired her. Whatever compensation she was getting, she deserved it. Once when I was at her house, she wore a sleeveless tee shirt. I saw a scar on the back of her shoulder that disappeared down her back. She noticed me staring at it and grinned. "One of my knife scars," she said without further explanation.

I wondered what Jessie would think of her.

Chapter 12

Forty-eight hours later, I drove once more onto Mickie's driveway. This time Jessie rode along with me. I hadn't heard anything new about the investigation into the deaths of her mother or her male friend. Jessie filled me in with one new item.

"They found mom's shoes in the house where they found the second victim. Josh thinks she tried to flee, but they found her. He thinks two people were involved with the killing. He said he didn't believe she suffered much."

"That's good," I said, thinking that's what Josh said to be kind. "Was there still furniture in that abandoned house?"

"I asked Josh that, too. He said there was. Everything was dusty, but the house was full of furniture."

"Odd."

"I guess so."

To my surprise, Mickie waited in the front yard.

"Is that her?"

"Yes, she usually lets her two dogs intimidate me for a while before she comes out. She's being nice because you're with me."

Jessie grinned and climbed out of my Mustang without showing a second thought about the dogs. I followed her and made the introduction. The two appeared to hit it off from the start.

"Wow! Is this all yours," Jessie said when we went inside, and she saw the working space with all the weapons or pieces of weapons.

"It's a hobby that pays the bills. Come, let's sit over here."

The room still only had the two chairs. Jessie sat down next to Mickie. When she realized there were only the two chairs, she looked at me and started to stand.

"Stay seated, Jessie, Jim's not staying. He'll just get in the way." Mickie looked at me, "We'll call you when she's finished."

I started to hand Mickie the small case that contained my Beretta, but she shook her head. "That's not the right weapon for her."

Jessie didn't protest, so I left. It didn't surprise me that I wasn't invited to stay. My presence would not have added any value to the lesson.

Three hours later, her call caught me working on the same section of the cinder block wall I had been trying to fix for the past week. When I arrived, I found them waiting in the front yard. Jessie knelt in front of the two boxers and appeared to be scratching behind the ears of both dogs.

Mickie simply nodded at me as Jessie opened the door to my car to get in. "That was fantastic. Thank you!" she said to me.

"Tell me what all happened," I said as I turned the car around. I didn't need to encourage her.

"She's amazing. Did you know she was in the Army?" Rather than give me a moment to answer, she continued. "I think she's missing part of her leg, the left one. She was in combat. She's married, but I think she likes you. Can you believe she asked me if you were hitting on me? I had to laugh at that. No offense. She said, 'Good, otherwise I'd have to shoot him.' I wouldn't want her as my enemy. She's like one of those women you see in those movies. Those dogs are so cute. She let me shoot this pistol of hers, and I got to be pretty good. We shot at cans, just like my old boyfriend did on his farm. She wants me to come back. I need to call her first, and she warned me to never come unannounced when it was dark. That did kind of scare me."

Once she finished rambling, I asked, "How many cans were you hitting by the time you finished?"

"I couldn't hit any at first, but at the end I was hitting four out of ten. She's an expert. When I got frustrated, she put out ten of those skinny cans and hit them all in about five seconds. She told me at first, she couldn't hit a can either. She said there was no reason to carry a gun if you weren't sure you would hit the target. She told me you could only hit five out of ten, and that's why you didn't carry. Is that right?"

"I don't carry a weapon, because I don't get into situations where I need one." It wasn't the biggest lie I ever told, but I rationalized it was one of my life's objectives I had failed miserably to achieve. "Besides, she was wrong, I can usually hit nine of the ten cans." The only stretch in that statement was the word usually.

Jessie grinned. "I think she likes you."

"Don't go there, I have a lady friend."

Jessie looked at me skeptically. "She asked me a lot of questions about my mom, my life, etc. At first, I thought she was just being chatty, but I sensed that she really wanted to know. Think she did?"

"I do. Despite the toughness, Mickie is a good person. She's had a tough life, been through a lot. I imagine she likes you, which is good. You don't want her as an enemy," I said, smiling, but I meant it.

Back at my house, Jessie thanked me again and left on her motorcycle still riding a high. I felt good about the day, but I did wonder if I was creating something that might come back and bite us all.

Josh stopped by the next day. He didn't tell me he was coming by, so his arrival struck me as curious. I offered to let him come inside, but he stayed on the front step.

"I wanted to come by to thank you for helping Jessie get a shooting lesson. I didn't know that lady lived out there. Jessie said she was a friend of yours."

"An acquaintance more than a friend."

"Do you know her story?"

"Her story?" I asked.

"She's a highly decorated veteran. Jessie and I checked her out on the internet last night. She's got tons of medals. She served twice in Afghanistan and got all messed up over there."

"Messed up?"

"Injured. I read that her group got attacked by a large group of Taliban. Nearly everyone died, that she got shot and stabbed. More than once they had to fight off the Taliban hand-to-hand. When a rescue team came in by helicopter, an explosion, I think it was from a grenade, but that may be wrong, anyway, the explosion took off part of her leg. She almost died. The man who got rescued with her said that none of them would have lasted as long as they did if it wasn't for her. He described her as a tigress defending her cubs. I want to meet her."

"Go easy on that. She likes to keep a low profile. To say she's a loner may be an understatement."

"The way Jessie described her had me thinking. I checked her out this morning but couldn't find anything negative about her in any of the databases I have access to."

"Josh, don't try to dig anything up on her. You'd be wasting your time and doing her a great disservice."

"I didn't plan on doing anything else. I was just curious and thought you might know more about her," Josh said.

"Come inside. I'll tell you everything I know."

He came in, and over the next ten minutes, I told him everything I knew about her. Telling it, I realized that I knew little more than he did. I stressed my belief that she wasn't doing anything wrong and wanted to be left alone. I was being paranoid, but Josh was a motivated, imaginative, rookie law enforcement officer. Conversely, Mickie wanted to remain a shadow in the dark.

"You have to admire her," he said when I finished.

"You do. Keep her existence a secret. She's not, of course, she pays taxes, buys groceries, etc., but she is indeed a curiosity. If you start telling your buddies, some deputy will want to go check her out officially." I used my fingers to display quotation marks when I said officially. "That could lead to some bad, unintentional consequences."

He nodded his head. "I see your point. I know of two guys I wouldn't want to tell."

I didn't ask him to elaborate. I did ask him how much time he was spending with Jessie. He blushed.

"I like her. Don't misunderstand, we're just friends. I worry about her, too. Did she tell you she wants me to help her pick out a dog."

"No, but I knew she wanted a dog. How is she doing, you know, living alone in that house?"

"I think alright. She has spent time at her aunt's house lately. We ordered a security system for her."

"Are you involved in the murder investigation?"

"Not as much as I would like. I help out here and there, and they do want me to be the main point of contact for Jessie. That's good."

"Any progress made yet that you can tell me about?" I asked.

"None really that I know of. They did talk to Mr. Cobb at the truck stop. He told them that the other victim, his name was Xavier Perkins, had stopped there for the night once or twice a month for the past couple of years. He drove one of those big eighteen wheelers cross country. Mrs. Perez usually picked him up at the truck stop and brought him back. He had no idea where they went."

"Has Jessie said anything more about someone watching or following her?"

"I've asked her about that, and she says no."

We talked for a few more minutes, and then he left. If I was a betting man, I'd happily bet my lunch that he was looking forward to spending more time with Jessie.

Chapter 13

Two days later, I had another unexpected contact with a deputy. Deputy Johnny Willis called me and asked me to meet him for coffee. I agreed, and upon his request for me to pick a spot, I suggested the donut shop.

He was waiting for me with a basket of donuts already on the small table. Nancy was standing next to him with a cup of coffee that she held out for me. Once I sat down, she left us.

"Thanks for coming by, Jim." He had some powdered sugar on the tip of his nose that had come from a powdered sugar donut. I wondered why Nancy hadn't mentioned it and wondered if I should.

"Not a problem, what can I do for you?"

"First, I'd like to apologize for getting you mixed up in all this."

"That wasn't you. I let that young lady get me involved."

"Yes, but I had the discussion with Mitch, Deputy Amon, about sending Josh out there to talk to her and encouraged Mitch to have Josh take you with him. Neither one of us ever thought things were going to turn out like they did."

"No reason why you should've."

"But it did, and I know both are still in contact with you."

"Infrequently, but yes." I wondered where this was going.

"We've done some additional digging and have been in contact with some federal agencies. What we've learned scares us a little." He paused to take a bite of donut. The donut must have brushed his nose again, and he wiped the end of his nose with a napkin. "Theory has it this Perkins guy may have transported stuff across country for a nasty group based in Miami. The Bureau has had him as a person of interest for over a year."

"Did he double cross them?"

"That's where it gets a little interesting. No one knows whether he double crossed the Miami group, or if some second group is involved. Something is missing that the Miami group is hunting for. It was supposed to be dropped off in Dallas, but it wasn't. Anyway, the underworld, if I can use that Hollywood term, is in an uproar."

"That's never good."

"No, it's not."

"Are the feds wanting to step in and take over the investigation?"

"No. Where it gets more interesting is that whatever it is that has gone missing, it wasn't anything illegal. At least that is what they are hearing and have passed on to us. It's something personal. It belonged to one of the bosses and was being transported to Dallas to be delivered to his daughter. The crate reached Dallas, but the item wasn't in there."

"And they thought the driver may have taken it," I said.

"One possibility. But get this, the crate supposedly had a ton of drugs in it, and the drugs arrived untouched."

"Why the driver?" I asked.

"They don't know, but apparently the big boss who sent the item is taking this theft very personal. A few other people involved in the packaging and delivering part of their business have turned up missing. There's been a little shake up in Dallas, too."

"I wouldn't want to be in their shoes. Any idea what this missing gift might be?"

"Not really, their best guess is that it's an expensive piece of jewelry that might have been in the family for a long time. I think the feds are receiving various bits of data from lower-level contacts they have inside the organization."

"Why package it with the drugs? That seems stupid."

"Who knows? Maybe he wanted to save on postage. These guys have access to private jets. He could've flown it to Dallas himself," Johnny said.

"So why tell all this to me?"

"Because it puts everything in a different perspective. It gives more credence to Ms. Perez' concern that someone was watching or following her. It also puts her and anyone else involved, like you, in a position where you may want to be a little more aware of what's going on around you."

"I'm too far out of her circle of acquaintances to be affected. How's Josh handling it?"

"I think he likes her, so he's concerned."

"They'd both be safer if he was inside the house. Although, I doubt if she is in any real danger," I said.

"We don't think so either. My coming here to tell you this is because it would be wrong not to. While none of us think you'll ever be targeted by them, we have an obligation to let you know what we've been told."

"Thanks."

"Besides, there is strong evidence that neither Perkins nor the woman were killed right away. They both had wounds inflicted before the fatal blow. Knowing now what we do, we believe someone was trying to get information about the missing item from them before killing them. At least, that's our working theory."

"Were there any drugs in the truck?"

"Unfortunately, we don't know for sure. We believe it was clean when it was here. If it had any, they were dropped off in Dallas as reported. Besides, the trucking company sent another driver. That driver and the truck were long gone before the bodies were discovered. It had been up and down the west coast, loaded and unloaded a couple of times. I think everyone felt by then there was no use to search it for any drugs.

I nodded but didn't feel a need to comment. I imagined having something personal stolen would anger a crime boss a lot more than if someone pilfered some of the drugs. Johnny didn't elaborate any further, and the conversation turned to golf, traveling, and women. All topics I often thought about but rarely followed up on.

He left first, saying he had a meeting to get to. I thanked him for the update and stayed to finish my coffee. I thought about what he had told me. If this had become personal to some big crime lord, it may not end quickly. I had experienced too many situations where people overreacted to what I thought wasn't a big deal. Almost always, those situations resulted from the person taking the transgression as personal.

Nancy walked over and sat down in the chair Deputy Willis had used. "Are you in trouble again?"

"Why do you always think the worst? Maybe he was here to give me another good citizen award."

She grinned, and a second later her smile faded. "It's a shame about that girl's mother. Was that what this was about?"

"Yes, he was just bringing me up to speed on a few things. He blames himself for sending me out to see the girl."

"Is that when the mom and that man were discovered? I heard about it on the news and couldn't help but think about you and the girl."

"Yep, not a pleasant memory."

"I can't imagine. How's the daughter doing? Remember, you mentioned her to me," she said.

I did. "She's hanging in there."

We talked about the donut business for a while, and I finally got her to thank me for singlehandedly keeping her in business. Before leaving, I asked her to tell her husband hello for me.

Chapter 14

"This is a waste of time," Carlos La Cruz growled to his partner.

"They said the reward was now twenty-five thousand dollars. How could this be a waste of time?" His partner, Victorio Pena, asked.

"I don't mean that, Vic. I meant him. He doesn't know anything."

Vic slapped the hooded man's head. "Is that so?" he asked the motionless man. He didn't get a response.

"You may have already killed him," Carlos said. He lifted the man's hood and studied the man's face. "I don't think he's going to tell us anything more."

"Let me see," Vic said and leaned in close. He reached into his pocket and removed a small pocket-knife. He used it to slice along the man's left cheek. Only a small amount of blood dribbled out. "Yeah, he's dead. Let me finish my beer, and we can dump him."

"Dammit, I wish you hadn't been so quick to kill the driver," Carlos said. "You could've saved us all this trouble."

"Yeah, me too, but you didn't do any better with the woman."

"That was an accident. I had a lot more planned for her, but she was a fighter. She went crazy on me. I didn't mean to snap her neck like that."

"You know, I doubt if the necklace got this far anyway. Hell, Cobb's place is just a truck-stop on the way west. My bet is that it never left Miami, or it's in Dallas. The driver probably didn't even know what he was transporting."

"Let's dump him and go back home to Roswell for a few days."

"Sounds like a plan," Vic said.

"You know, if we find this necklace, my guess is it's worth a lot more than the reward. Maybe we should keep it."

"I can't imagine what they'd do to us if they caught us with it. They'd skin us alive if they found out we were just thinking about stealing it. Let's stick with the reward, brother."

Earlier that evening, the two men had lured Chester Cobb to a truck in the very back of his truck stop. Once there, they had forced him into their van and had driven him to an old abandoned house west of Portales. They were not very good interrogators, but they were brutal. They hadn't learned much from him, and they figured he was probably being truthful when he said he didn't have any knowledge of the missing necklace. He barely knew Perkins, having only met him a handful of times when he parked his big rig for the night at the truck stop.

Cobb knew the woman Perkins was with and had told them what he could about her. He admitted he had had sex with the woman a dozen or so times over the years. He described her as a prostitute who worked the truck stop, hitting on the drivers. If she struck out with them, he claimed he could always get her on a discount.

He said he doubted if Perkins would have told the woman anything about any illegal activities he may have been involved in. Cobb didn't know of anyone else in Melrose with whom Perkins may have associated.

They tossed Cobb back into the van after removing his wallet.

The two split the hundred and eighteen dollars they found in the wallet. Halfway to Roswell, they left the body in a shed behind another abandoned, rundown house. Over the years the two men had located dozens of abandoned houses, gas stations, and other small buildings along this route. In their line of work, knowledge of these places came in handy.

"I hate to give up on this," Carlos said. The lights of Roswell could be seen in the distance. "I don't think the necklace is there, but maybe we should search the woman's house. We can do it when the girl is away." Before he died, Cobb had told them about the daughter and had given them pretty good directions to her house.

"Might be more fun to do it while she is there. Besides, she might know something," Vic said.

"Let's give it a week or so. No reason to take the risk if the necklace pops up somewhere else. Cobb's disappearance is going to heat things up there for a while. Maybe we should give it two weeks to cool down."

"I don't think we should wait that long. If she has the necklace, she may try to sell it or do something else stupid. Cobb said she was around twenty years old. We won't have to worry about social services moving in and finding it, but still, I don't think we should wait too long."

Vic and Carlos had met as teenagers on the back streets of Las Cruces, New Mexico. They had a common interest in terrorizing the other kids in the city. They were both taller and larger than most of the other teenagers. They were also a lot more brutal than most.

Neither had any respect for authority and ran afoul of the law as well as the few street gangs in the city. They formed their own gang while staying away from the turf of the established gangs in the city. Once the two thought they were strong enough they savagely attacked and killed the leader and two lieutenants of one of the smaller established gangs. They absorbed the other gang members into their group. In doing so, they more than doubled the size of their own street gang.

Within a year they were waging a full-fledged gang war in Las Cruces. The violence and bloodshed forced the city police to move in and arrest several gang members. Carlos and Vic were two of those who soon found themselves serving hard time in one of the state penitentiaries. Four years later, they were both back out on the streets more dangerous and more connected than ever with the criminal organizations that operated country-wide.

Through contacts they had made in prison, the two young men were able to market themselves as outside contractors to several of the larger criminal organizations in the country. Over the years, they developed a dependable and ruthless reputation. They rarely had face to face meetings with their employers. Business was conducted in emails and over the phone. Payments were handled via bank transfers.

Their semi-legitimate source of income came from running the largest temporary services company in Roswell for blue collar workers. Immigrants, mostly legal, who arrived in Roswell looking for work routinely found employment through them. Construction companies, landscape companies, janitorial services, and other similar enterprises would reach out to them for employees.

Despite their ruthless nature, they played fair with their clients and their employees. Vic had a cousin, Lara, whom they employed as their office manager. They paid her well and let her run the company. Within the first year, Lara needed three other employees to help her in the office.

Lara knew about Vic's and Carlos' past, but had no knowledge of their ongoing criminal activities. She didn't want to know. She suspected the gas explosion that eliminated their only real competition shortly before she was hired may not have been an accident, but she never spoke about it.

For their part, Vic and Carlos almost never went to the office. Lara would meet with them for dinner once or twice a week at Vic's favorite steak house. During these dinners, she would brief them on any significant issues. These were rare and usually involved one of their clients failing to make a payment. A visit by the duo to the client usually remedied the problem.

The two had often discussed the similarity of their temporary services company to the individual who occasionally hired them to fulfill various tasks for unidentified clients. Just as a construction or cleaning company might reach out to them looking for someone who could help fill their labor needs for a specific project, their primary contact, whom they only knew as Jack, had customers who reached out to him. The main difference was the nature of the work. What Carlos and Vic specialized in included assassination, recovery, and collection. Death being the common denominator.

The current task had been short notice. Jack had requested they determine if Xavier Perkins had swiped a necklace from a major player in Miami. He didn't need to elaborate on what he meant by major player. Both Vic and Carlos understood.

If Perkins had it, they were to retrieve the necklace. The killing of Perkins, and subsequently Perez and Cobb, had not been requested or included in the task. Of course, all parties knew without specific instructions to the contrary, someone dying was to be expected.

The twenty-five thousand dollar reward was at the lower end of their normal payments and only guaranteed if they located the necklace. They might not have taken the job, except they thought it to be good business to be responsive to Jack. They also wanted to ingratiate themselves with his customer. It never hurt to have the gratitude of any person highly placed in the world of organized crime.

Jack had assured them if the necklace was recovered elsewhere, he would inform them. They had no reason to doubt his word. He had provided them sufficient information to allow them to be waiting for Perkins when he pulled into Cobb's truck stop. They searched the truck while Perkins and his lady friend ate dinner at a cheap looking diner next door. They did a thorough search of the inside of the cabin where the driver and any passengers would sit. Failing to find what they were looking for there, they did a cursory check of the trailer looking for a gym bag or suitcase.

Not finding it didn't surprise them. Perkins could easily have it in a pocket of his pants. He could have already sold it or given it away, maybe to the woman he was with in the diner. The possibility that he never had the necklace didn't matter.

They watched Perkins and the woman walk out of the diner hugging and laughing. When Perkins drove away in the woman's van, they followed it.

Chapter 15

Five days after my conversation with Deputy Willis, he again called me. After apologizing for interrupting my morning, he asked if I would meet him at the same donut shop. I had already devoured a bowl of cheerios for my breakfast, but I told him I would. He suggested we meet in fifteen minutes. I skipped shaving, put on a clean shirt, and was out the door with five minutes to spare.

Johnny sat at the same table we used before. I saw a basket of donuts and two coffee cups on the table.

"I could get used to this. Are you treating again?"

"Yes. I need to talk to you." He looked serious.

"Am I in trouble?"

"No. Did you ever talk to Chester Cobb? He managed the truck stop in Melrose. It's the only one."

"I remember the name, I think, but I never met or talked to him. Why? What's up?"

"We didn't think so." He took a sip of coffee and looked down into the cup like he was trying to decide what to say next.

"Something happen to him?"

"He's disappeared. Josh said you were with him when the old man, you know, the one who discovered Jessie's mom, recommended we talk to Cobb. It was a long shot, but we wanted to know if you talked to him, and whether he may have told you something that he didn't tell us later."

"No, sorry. Never went near him."

"Don't be. I didn't think you had, but we're grasping at straws. Cobb claimed his only connection with the two victims was that she met Perkins at the truck stop and took him somewhere each night he stopped there. They've been doing that for the past several months, maybe the past year."

"Think Cobb was involved with the murders and is now trying to disappear?"

"No. It's one theory, but we have pretty much discounted it. A review of the truck stop's security cameras showed him heading to the back of the lot with another man three nights ago and never returning. We have not been able to identify this other man. We also have a plain white van leaving from the back area a few seconds later. The plates were dirty. We think he was abducted."

"Interesting," I said.

"Apparently, he occasionally had sex with the Perez woman at the truck stop, too. An assistant manager was more than happy to tell us. She thought Cobb was a jerk."

"My guess is that whoever is trying to find the missing jewelry, or whatever it is, has just expanded their search."

"We hope that's not the case," Johnny said.

I thought I knew what he meant. If whoever was behind this kept grabbing people in Melrose, it wouldn't be long before Jessie became a target.

"How's Josh handling it?" I asked.

"You mean beyond having a nervous breakdown."

"That bad?"

"No, and I shouldn't have said that. He has a two-day course he needs to attend that started today. He argued like hell to be allowed to take it later. It took a direct order and a threat of being fired to get him to go."

"He's nervous about Jessie, right?"

"Absolutely," Johnny said.

"Is he at the class?"

"Thankfully," he nodded his head. "This class is the sheriff's big priority. If I was a disgruntled employee, I could tell you what a waste of time the class is, but since I'm not, I won't."

I grinned.

"Would you mind driving out there and checking on her? Just for a few seconds, you wouldn't have to stay or anything. On the few occasions we've had a patrol go by, she simply says she's fine. She might open up to you, and it may placate Josh. We're already two deputies short, and I'd hate to lose him."

"No problem. She's been on my mind lately, too."

"Thanks, Jim. I need to run. Will you give me a shout on your way back?"

"Of course."

Johnny's quick departure made me think he wanted to leave before I had a chance to change my mind.

"Did you make him mad?" Nancy asked. She carried a pot of coffee and refilled my cup.

"No, why would you ask?"

"He left in a hurry and forgot to pay for the donuts and coffee."

"No way," I said. "Well, he's probably good for it."

Nancy didn't move. She stared at me and lifted her hand, palm up.

"You want me to pay?"

"No matter how much it hurts."

When I left a few minutes later, Nancy was still smiling. My getting stuck with the bill somehow seemed to make her day. I drove off wondering if getting me to check on Jessie was Johnny's real motive for talking to me. The questions about Cobb did seem relevant, but I sensed a real concern for Jessie.

I didn't need to check my calendar. I knew the next thing on it was an oil change, and that wasn't until next week. Chubbs needed more dog food, so I stopped by a grocery store on my way home. I had some time to kill before I planned on calling Jessie.

Jessie answered her phone on the second ring. "Hi, Jim, how are you doing?"

"Fine, are you free if I come out to visit?"

"Now?"

"It'll take me a half hour. I'd like to buy you lunch."

"Sounds great. I'm at the Richardson's ranch right now. Can you come by here?"

I told her I could, and she sent me the address. She said she'd tell the Richardsons and call me back if she couldn't get away.

The ranch stood out from the natural terrain that surrounded it. Decades ago, the Richardsons or whoever owned the property planted several trees on the ranch. For whatever reason I have never fully understood, trees didn't simply pop up and grow in this part of New Mexico like they did in most parts of the country. A bunch of trees usually indicated there was a house nearby. Three buildings that I imagined were stables or storage buildings sat about a hundred yards north of the main house.

A fence with a gate ran around the property in front of the house. The gate was open, so I drove in. As I neared the house, I saw Jessie and two adults standing off to the left by what I thought was a corral. A lone horse stood inside the corral right next to the people.

Jessie waved at me, and I drove closer to them before parking. All three walked toward me as I climbed out of the car.

"Hi, Jim," Jessie called out.

I smiled and nodded at the three.

"This is Nate and Bella Richardson," Jessie said.

Nate and I shook hands. He might have been an inch taller than my six feet. His short cropped grey hair made me think he also had me by a few years. Bella gave me a once over with her big, brown eyes. "So, I understand you're taking our Jessie to lunch?" she asked.

"First class," I said.

Nate snorted and grinned. "Not around here."

"Jessie, could you take Star back inside. We'll keep Jim company until you return," Bella said.

"Sure, I'll be right back, Jim." Jessie hopped the fence, scratched Star's throat, and started walking toward the corral gate. The big horse followed her.

"She's really amazing with the horses," Bella said, watching Jessie. "Forgive us for asking, but what is your role in all this?" She turned to face me when she asked. Her eyes stared into mine, and I got the impression this wasn't a simple, friendly question.

"I don't know if I have a role. She approached me out of the blue to ask for help in finding her mom. I didn't want to get involved, but I did. I came out with a young deputy to see her a day or two later and was with him when we discovered the body. I mean bodies. I haven't seen much of her since then, so I thought I would check up on her today."

"You're helping her learn how to shoot. That seems like you're more involved than you say," Bella said.

Nate jumped into the conversation. He likely noticed that Bella had gotten under my skin. "Jim, we are overly protective of Jessie. We've known her since she was a little thing. She's been working here for over six years, and Bella's been like a mother to her. Better than her real one, that's for sure. We are worried about her, frightened really. Please understand our concern."

"I do. I'm worried, too. So is a young deputy."

"Josh?" Bella asked.

"Yes."

"She likes him," Bella said.

"I believe the feeling is mutual."

"She likes you, too."

I looked at Bella for a second, trying to figure out what she meant with that remark. "I like her, too, but not in the way Josh probably does. There is not and will not be anything developing like that between us."

"I didn't mean that," Bella said, but her eyes continued to stare into mine, and I knew they carried a warning. "We've offered to have her move in with us, but she likes her own place. Guess I would've too at her age."

"You live in Clovis?" Nate asked in an obvious attempt at changing the topic. I told him I did, and we talked about the changes in Clovis over the years. "Have you been to the new museum?"

"What museum?"

"The High Plains Historical Museum? It's at the fairgrounds," he said. "My best friend's uncle is mentioned in a placard there."

Bella wandered off in the direction Jessie went.

"I'll have to check it out."

Once Bella was far enough away that she wouldn't hear us,

Nate took a step closer to me. "We weren't the biggest fans of Jessie's mom. Four years ago, a man Anita brought home, you know, one of her customers, her Johns, assaulted Jessie in her bedroom. Her screaming and fighting luckily made the man stop, and Anita did eventually sober up enough to realize what was happening. The two chased the man out of the house."

"Jessie was okay?"

"Fortunately," he nodded. "When Bella found out about it, she went immediately to confront Anita. She didn't tell me she was going. She told Anita in no uncertain terms that if she ever brought another man home, she would kill her. Luckily, we didn't have to find out if she would have. As far as we knew, Anita never brought a man home again."

"Bella and Jessie talk that much?"

He grinned, "All the time. I can only imagine what all she's told Jessie about me."

Chapter 16

Jessie stretched out in the passenger seat. Her Eastern New Mexico Greyhounds tee shirt rode up and exposed a part of her belly. "You should put the roof down."

"Your wish is my command," I said. I waited for the roof to recede before driving away from the ranch.

Jessie waved at the Richardsons. I noticed a young man with jet black hair leaning against the side wall of the house watching us leave.

"Who's the guy with the black hair by your motorcycle?"

Jessie looked back. "Oh, he's a creep. He's a nephew or something. He's supposed to be helping out, but I never see him doing anything. Bella says to ignore him. He won't be here much longer. I think there may be something wrong with him."

I didn't say anything.

"You know there's no place to eat around here. There's a hamburger place by the school that's not too bad," she said.

"Then a hamburger it is."

She gave me directions, and in less than ten minutes, we parked in the small parking lot of the restaurant. A half dozen pickups occupied most of the parking spots. I found one at the far left of the lot.

On the ride to the restaurant, Jessie had talked about my car, how she would like to own a convertible, and how much she liked Star. She said the Richardson's owned a dozen horses, but Star was her favorite.

She seemed to be oblivious to the danger she was in. The luxury of innocence, I thought. A great thing while it lasted. I imagined I had been young and innocent once, thinking the whole world was a playground. Somewhere, that world changed, or maybe it was me.

The inside of the restaurant looked clean and orderly. Most of the tables were occupied, and it appeared that red plastic baskets with a pile of French fries or with a burger wrapped in paper were the local favorites. I didn't see a menu.

"Hi Jessie, the usual today?" said a heavy-set man wearing a white apron covered with grease stains. He wore wire rimmed glasses and his white hair appeared to be losing the battle with baldness.

"Yes, Mr. T. How are you today?"

"You know, life's a song," he said, smiling at her.

She giggled. An inside joke, I thought.

"We have hamburgers and cheeseburgers. What's your poison?" he said looking at me.

"A hamburger, please."

"Gotcha," he said and walked away.

I looked at Jessie. "What does one drink here?"

"Follow me," she said.

She led me across the room to a soft drink dispenser. A stack of clean plastic cups sat next to it. The cups came in one size only, large. She took a cup, filled it halfway with crushed ice, and topped it off with root beer. I copied her but filled my glass with diet Dr. Pepper.

"You can get refills," she said as we sat down. "Mr. T. will bring us a basket of French fries with our burgers."

"Sounds like a good system. How come you're so popular?"

She grinned. "I've been coming here for years." She looked around like she wanted to make sure no one was listening. "Want to know something that you have to keep secret?"

"I don't know."

"That guy you pointed out by my motorcycle at the ranch, his name is Shawn. The more I think about it, I think he may be the person who was following me around those few days after my mom disappeared. I'm not sure, so I don't want to get him into any trouble."

"Why would he be following you around?"

She blushed. "I think he likes me. He's always watching me at the ranch. I've tried to talk to him, but he always walks away. I think he may have been the person who went inside my house that one day, too."

"Don't you think the police should know?"

"I mentioned it to Bella. She said she would take care of it. Later, she said I didn't have to worry about Shawn anymore. Bella can be tough. If she talked to Shawn, you can be sure he won't be following me around anymore."

"You like her?"

"Yes. Way back when I started working there, Bella worked with me all day. She called me her little apprentice. I had to look up that word. She worked with me for two years, and then she said I was on my own. She promoted me."

"How did you start working there?"

"I passed the ranch on the school bus every day. One day I decided to get off and just ask her if I could help."

"And she said yes?"

"Not at first, but when I told her who I was, she changed her mind."

I thought I knew what she meant. Word gets around, especially in small towns. Bella likely knew about Jessie's mom.

"I think you should tell Josh about Shawn," I said.

"I don't know. He's still a boy."

"Shawn?"

"No, Josh. I'm afraid he would want to rush out and confront Shawn."

"You like Josh?"

"Yes, but don't tell him that. He needs to work through that himself."

"I won't tell him, but are you sure Shawn's no threat?"

"I think he has some kind of learning disability. You know what I mean?"

"I think so." I knew that didn't make him harmless, but I kept my thoughts to myself.

"He's only going to be here another week or so. Bella told me this was like a vacation for him. He's been there before, but only for a few days at a time. This is the longest he has stayed here. He still lives with his family in Colorado."

"How would he know where you live?"

"He can drive and does the feed run to the tractor store. Nate gives him a note listing what all they need, and I guess he does okay. Nate has also taught him to drive the tractor and move the hay bales."

I wondered why she had earlier said that she'd never seen him do anything. "Does he have a car?"

"No, but the Richardson's have two old cars they park behind the stables. Shawn could've borrowed one of them. I think one of those is what he takes to the tractor store."

"How's the dog hunt going?" I asked to change the topic.

"It's kind of on hold. Josh thinks I need a car if I'm going to take care of a dog. I can't afford a car."

"I guess that makes sense. At least, until you could teach the dog to ride with you on your bike." I grinned as I said this.

"We talked about that. I've seen them do that on television, but Josh didn't think that was practical. I reminded him that he has a car."

"But he didn't take the hint?"

"No. I'm not sure he wants to."

"My guess is that he is not sure what you want, or maybe he's not sure what the proper thing is for him to do. Do you want him to move in with you?"

"He needs to figure that out on his own."

"And it's none of my business, I know."

She grinned, and the arrival of our hamburgers rescued me from any further discussion on the topic. Jessie devoured her hamburger and half the French fries so fast I wondered if she hadn't eaten much in the last day or two.

As we waited for the check, Jessie leaned in and whispered, "I'm becoming a good shot. I've been back to Mickie's twice since you took me."

"Good for you," I said, wondering really if that was a good thing. Personally, I think people should become proficient with guns and especially with gun safety. However, I certainly understand the argument against them. "Do you have one?"

"Not yet. Josh wants me to wait until I'm nineteen."

"And that will be?"

"Next week."

"Well, happy birthday."

"Thanks."

On the way out of the restaurant, she paused to look at a poster sized photo of the most recent Melrose High School football team. "We won state. I had already graduated, but I knew all the guys."

I imagined she did.

During the drive back to the ranch, she reassured me that she was safe. She hadn't seen anything suspicious lately, and she had purchased new locks for her house. Josh was coming over on Saturday to install the new security system.

I didn't see the Richardsons or Shawn when I dropped Jessie off. She said thanks, waved, and jogged off toward the stables.

Jessie could have had her mom's car, but for obvious reasons, she never wanted to see it again. I couldn't blame her. Josh had mentioned to me that a used car dealer had bought it from her for pennies on the dollar.

Chapter 17

Half asleep, Mickie groaned and rolled over in her bed. She sensed the beginning of her nightmare. She tried, as she always did, to fend it off. As usual, the dream came anyway.

In her dream, as in real life, the explosion caught her by surprise. It caught them all by surprise. The sound of automatic gunfire that followed the explosion did not surprise them. They responded like the well-honed team they were.

"Where are they?" her lieutenant had asked.

She scanned the hilly area around them. The dust from the explosion blurred her vision and tried to choke her.

"East about three hundred yards in the rocks on the side of the hill." The response came back over the radio from Froggy, one of the three men on their perimeter.

"Injuries?"

Silence.

The sun had started its climb in the east behind their attackers.

"We need to move," Mickie said. She wanted to scream this out loud, but she remembered she spoke in a calm voice.

They did move, and unlike the start of the dream, the next forty hours rushed through her mind as it usually did. Dead and severely injured faces, both American and Taliban, stared up at her at random. She could remember the faces, all of them, despite her repeated efforts to forget. Hour after hour her team retreated. All the while, they were slowly dying. They killed ten Taliban for each life lost, but the enemy kept coming. Like fire ants, she thought.

Two aborted rescue attempts left them on their own to fight and survive. Salvaging ammunition and water from their own dead allowed them to last as long as they did. They even took ammunition and weapons from the dead Taliban who made the mistake of getting too close.

In her dream, she could still smell the foul breath of the enemy soldier who sliced and stabbed her. She never knew who on her team shot her attacker, killing him before he could fatally wound her. Another enemy soldier jumped her as soon as that one fell back and died. She fought back, and her knife struck first.

At some point, Mickie believed, the enemy had made the mistake of wanting to capture the last of the Americans rather than kill them. Maybe it was just her they wanted. A political prize for sure, she thought. An ambitious goal, one that was too ambitious due to the circumstances. Like a large pack of hyenas underestimating a smaller pride of lions.

Although injured, Mickie was able to help Froggy limp away, leaving over a dozen dead bodies behind. Two other soldiers supported each other and followed Mickie and Froggy. In her dream for some reason, she couldn't remember who they were.

The four of them stumbled on. The enemy regrouped. A few hours later, she saw fifteen to twenty more Taliban closing in on them from the north. Knowing they couldn't move fast enough to get away, the four Americans found the best defensive position they could and waited. The enemy would have to pass through an open area to reach them. This would be their killing zone.

Her dream had moments of clarity but was mostly a blur. This scene always came at the end of her dream and was unusually vivid.

Lying on the ground, protected by a large rock that jutted up a few feet, she emptied her weapon on their attackers. At least four of them fell to the ground, yet they kept coming. She looked over at Froggy, who had found a position next to her. Had he fired a shot? She reached over to shake him. She never knew if he had already died. In her dream, this was where the bright light of the final explosion would normally wake her with a start.

However, this time, for the first time in many years, an explosion didn't wake her. She shook Froggy, and he rolled over. She gasped and woke up. The vison in her nightmare was not of Froggy. Rather, Jessie's face and lifeless eyes stared back into her own.

Mickie sat up in the darkness. Sweat covered her body. The nightmare came less often in the recent years. Her online therapist from the VA had told her it would never go away for good, but would ideally become a rarity. It had. She believed she could handle the dreams and had done quite well in shaking them off.

Not this one. This one was different. She couldn't let this one happen.

Chapter 18

Feeling that I had done my duty in checking up on Jessie, I felt pretty good on my way back. Her remark about Josh having to figure out on his own how much she liked him and whether he should move in with her made me smile. Most guys, myself included, are totally lost at figuring out what a woman wants. We need to be told and sometimes twice.

When I got home, I called Johnny and told him about my morning and lunch with Jessie. We both acknowledged there was not much to gain from it, but it was the right thing to do. He suggested I text Josh and let him know she was doing fine. I did and was not surprised when I received a thumbs up emoji from Josh seconds later.

The call I received the following day did surprise me.

"Jim, I need you to come see me this afternoon. Can you?" Mickie asked.

"Sure, what's up?"

"I'd rather discuss it when you get here."

"How soon?"

"Now if that's possible."

I agreed to come right out. Mickie had never summoned me before, and while I don't usually like being summoned, the fact that she appeared to need me for something intrigued me. I usually see her three or four times a year. This visit would equal that in less than a month.

She met me out in front of her house. Another first, I thought.

Her two beasts sat next to her and didn't come barking when my car stopped.

"Thanks for coming out," she said to me as I approached her. "Let's go inside."

She led me to a room that I had never been in. It looked like a normal dining room with a table and six chairs. A China hutch sat against a wall.

"Don't look so surprised. I can be normal, too."

"I never thought otherwise."

"And don't get your hopes up, I'm not making dinner."

I didn't respond. I figured she had a basement full of survival meals.

"What can I do for you?" I asked.

"Sit down and tell me everything you can about what happened to Jessie's mom and this so-called boyfriend of hers."

"I don't know much."

"You don't know much about anything, I know." Her sarcasm came out loud and clear. "Please just tell me what you do know or believe. I'm trying to piece a few things together. I'll share."

For the next fifteen minutes I told her everything I could remember. She stopped me a few times and asked for more detail. She didn't write anything down.

"What do you know about this Cobb character?" she asked.

"That he's gone missing. They think he was abducted and that his abduction might be related. I would've mentioned him, but you asked about her mom."

"His abduction has to be related. I'm sure he's dead by now," she said.

"What all do you know?"

"I've let myself get attached to Jessie. She reminds me of me when I was her age. Big differences but very similar, too. I reached out to some contacts I have to see what I could find out. As you can imagine, people with my background are sought after by a variety of legitimate and illegitimate entities. The man behind all this is Mario Pascual. He's one of the biggest players in the country. It was his necklace that went missing, and he's extremely pissed. His daughter, the one who was supposed to receive the necklace, is a nasty one, too. She's also not happy. Between the two, a lot of heads have rolled."

"Not a happy thought." I tried to hide my surprise regarding how much she had learned on her own.

"No. They've got a reward out for the necklace, and a few freelance killers are looking for it. The money is not much, but all these guys know what recovering the necklace means to Pascual. A chance to fall in the big guy's favor would be worth a lot more."

"You think one of these guys killed her mother and the others."

"Yes. From what you told me, the feds likely believe it, too," she said. "Hired killers are a dime a dozen. It's sad to say it, but it's true. Several teenage gangbangers grow up and become worse. Killing someone means absolutely nothing to them."

"You're preaching to the choir," I said.

"I know. My point is that Jessie is an obvious target for these guys. Follow their trail. Since the necklace wasn't found in Miami or Dallas, Perkins had to be considered the possible thief. Of course, the necklace could still be in one of those places or in Mobile."

"Mobile?" I said, interrupting her.

"It was the first stop out of Miami. People have died there, too."

I nodded. "So, Pascual has people in each of these cities he can reach out to?"

"I imagine he does, but that's not how it always works. There are a few individuals in the country who work independently as middlemen. They serve as a cut-out. That's normally whom someone like Pascual would reach out to. That person contracts with the local muscle. No one meets face to face. No direct links."

"How do you know all this stuff? You have a Facebook group?" I was trying to be funny, but Mickie didn't smile.

"I'm not on social media. I have email but block everything except for emails from a few contacts. Those are people I served with and, of course, my family."

"I don't blame you."

"My point is, Jim, the people here who are looking for the necklace aren't going to stop. They will continue to follow the leads they have. They went from Perkins, to Anita, to Cobb. The next logical step is Jessie and the house. They won't care that she's just a kid. They won't believe her right away when she pleads ignorance. They'll do whatever they want to her until they get the necklace or are satisfied that she doesn't know where it is. Then they will kill her."

"You don't think they may already realize the necklace isn't in Melrose?"

"They may think that, but they won't stop until they are sure. She may be their last victim, but that's too late."

I knew she was right. "So, what do we do?"

"We can try to convince her to stay at her aunt's house for the next couple of weeks. Hope they search her house, don't find it, and leave her alone."

"I don't like to rely on hope."

"Me neither, and this guy or guys, my bet there's two of them, are not nice. The bastards may look forward to interrogating Jessie. She'll just disappear one day, like Cobb did. They wanted Perkins to be found. Proof the job was done. Delivering him to Miami wasn't practical. Anita was collateral and didn't matter. From here until they are finished, they won't want their victims to be found."

"You've been giving this a lot of thought," I said.

"I'm obsessed with this damn situation. It's not good for me. I hold you responsible for bringing that girl into my life. We can't let something happen to her. It took me years to get over my first bout of depression."

"I can ask the sheriff to put a detail out there full time. They have to be considering such a step already. Plus, there's Josh."

"Talk to the sheriff. Anything will help, but these killers are pros. I need you to spend more time with her. Anywhere is fine. Your place, her place, the zoo, I don't care. Tell Josh to spend more time with her. Hell, she thinks she loves the guy. Tell him to have her move in with him."

"You know, neither one of them is going to listen to me."

"Just try."

"What are you going to do?"

"Besides using you? I'm going to keep digging to try to identify the killer or killers."

"And, if you find out who they are?"

"I haven't decided. Will you spend more time with her?"

"If she'll let me."

"Thanks. Keep your eyes open." She stood up.

I took that as my signal to leave. I stood, and we walked out to the front yard. She thanked me again for coming out.

"I'll stay in touch," I said as I climbed into my car.

My mind worked overtime on the drive home. I didn't like her telling me what I needed to do, but she had a point. I also wondered about her. I never knew very much about her past. I didn't know she had suffered from depression; however, seeing your whole team killed around you, as she did, could certainly cause it. The "survivor syndrome," I thought that's what I'd heard it called. Your mind has a hard time understanding why you survived when all your team members, many of them friends, died. In her mind, Jessie had now become another member of her team.

While I was there, I should have suggested Mickie invite Jessie to stay with her for a week or so. Neither one would have gone for it, and Mickie would've likely countered by suggesting Jessie move into my place. Touche, I thought. We'd better stick with pushing her at her aunt or Josh.

A car began following me as I neared my house. It looked like a small Kia and not threatening, but its windows had been darkened. The car followed me onto my street. I couldn't see the driver or how many people might be in the small car. Normally it wouldn't have bothered me, but after my conversation with Mickie, I was a little jumpy.

I turned onto my driveway and immediately hit my garage opener. I stepped out of my car just as the Kia pulled into my driveway.

Chapter 19

"Hi! I'm glad I caught up with you," Jessie's aunt said once she climbed out of the small car. "So, this is where you live."

"Yep, this is it. How are you today?"

"Excellent. Can I come in and talk to you about something?"

"I have a dog." The words came out of my mouth before I gave the question any thought.

"I know. Jessie said it was the sweetest thing. I'm not afraid of dogs."

My reluctance to ask her in made no real sense. "Please, come in."

She followed me in through the garage door. Chubbs didn't greet us. That surprised me, but I imagined he was asleep somewhere and didn't yet realize I had brought a guest into his domain.

"From the outside your house looks twice as big as mine."

"It's more than I need. Would you like some coffee or a coke?"

"No, thank you. I wanted to bring this to you rather than mail it." She handed me an envelope.

The envelope only had two names on it: mine as the addressee and Vicky Perez as the sender. I felt an instant sense of relief. Before reading it, I couldn't recall her first name.

"Please open it."

I did and inside discovered an invitation to a birthday party for Jessie.

"I'm having a small birthday party for Jessie. Can you believe she's going to be nineteen? My little Jessie. You have to come. She's insisting."

"Who's going to be there?"

"Just a few people. You and me, Jessie, her friend Josh, and possibly her friend Yvette. It's going to be simple, but she needs to have a party. These last few months have been hard on her."

I looked back down at the card. "Next Friday night," I said.

"I hope you're free. You must come."

I knew I was. "I can't imagine why she would want me to come to her birthday party. She'd probably prefer you invite the Richardsons."

"They're doing a lunch thing for her. No, she wants you there."

"Okay," I said.

"I'm glad all this investigation is over. I mean it's sad what happened to Nita, but now we can put it all behind us."

"The killers still need to be caught," I said.

"Yes, of course, but it no longer involves us. We can go on with our lives. The rodeo is this week. Do you ever go?"

"I have on a number of occasions." Curry county has an annual rodeo that is very well organized and run.

"We should go. I really enjoy it," Vicky said.

The "we" in her statement caught me off guard. "This year won't be good for me. I need to go down to the Cloudcroft area and look at some property. I'm already committed." A complete lie, but I thought I pulled it off well.

"Oh, that's too bad. I'd still like the opportunity to show you how appreciative I am for helping Jessie."

"I know you are, and that's enough."

"We'll see. I guess I better get going. Sorry, I didn't get to see your dog. Maybe next time," she said.

"What would be a good gift for Jessie?" I asked as I walked her out to her car.

"Who knows? Get her a gift card. That's what I'm doing. That way she can buy whatever she wants for herself."

"Okay. I'll see you next Friday."

Vicky gave a little wave and drove off. I stood there and wondered how I could manage to duck out of the birthday party early. Her comment that she was glad the matter with Nita was over popped back into my mind. I wondered if I should've contradicted her. On the one hand, it wasn't my place to tell her what the deputies had shared with me, but on the other, by knowing, she could help hide Jessie until this thing blew over.

I went back inside to look for Chubbs. He normally came out to inspect any visitors I have, and the fact that he hadn't concerned me. I found him lying on my bedroom floor. He didn't look up when I called his name. Kneeling next to him, I could hear his labored breathing. I saw some liquid next to his mouth on the floor.

There may have been a time, long ago, I would've simply ensured he was comfortable and waited out to see whatever happened next. Instead, I picked him up as gently as I could and took him out to my car. Together we headed to his veterinarian.

Once there, a young assistant took me to a back room and had me place Chubbs on a mat on the floor. She asked me a half dozen questions and then sent me out to the waiting area. I found a soft chair in the corner of the room. One other older man sat by himself in the room. He looked to be dozing.

A minute later, the assistant approached me. "The doctor will be seeing Chubbs in a minute. I have a couple questions. We have his name spelled two different ways. We have it with one b and with two bs. Which way is correct?"

"Either way is fine. He can't read, and neither one of us is particular."

She smiled again at me, but I thought I saw a lot of frustration and fatigue behind those eyes. "We do need to be correct. What is on his dog tags?"

"Let's go with two b's," I said. I knew she didn't need to be wasting her time with me.

"Two b's it is."

As she walked away, I wondered if my perspective on things had gotten more out of whack over the years. Chubbs, a dog, couldn't sign any legal documents, and more than likely had no preference how we spelled his name. When called, the pronunciation of his name wasn't affected by the number of b's. He didn't wear a collar unless I took him for a walk or brought him to see the vet. He wasn't allowed to roam free. To be honest, I may have spelled it differently time to time depending on how I felt at the moment.

Yet, I knew it wasn't the assistant's fault. Everything had to conform to the official files. I knew of more than one person who had trouble tracking down their own birth certificate, because their name had been informally changed by the parent as a child.

"Well, hello there."

I looked up and saw Nancy from the donut shop.

"Did I wake you up?" she asked.

"No, I was just daydreaming."

"Is your dog okay?"

"A bit under the weather. I hope that's all."

"Oh, that's too bad. I just brought Felix in for his regular checkup."

"Nancy, what does one buy for a nineteen-year-old girl for her birthday?"

"What? Why are you buying a teenager anything? No, wait, is it for that girl whose mother was killed?"

"Yes, her aunt is throwing her a small party and is insisting I come. I'm serious, what should I buy her."

"If you want something romantic—."

"No, I don't. Quit kidding me," I said, interrupting her.

She grinned. "Okay, in all seriousness, get her a gift card. Let her buy herself what she wants. That's all anyone does anymore."

"That's what her aunt said, too."

"How many adults are going to be there?"

"I think just me and her aunt."

"Her aunt single?" she asked.

"Yes."

"Oh, you poor man. She has plans for you. Best wear clean underwear."

"I hope not," I said, but I had already thought of that.

"Is she that bad? I've heard most single guys aren't that particular."

"No, she isn't that bad. I'm just not interested."

"Well, just have all your excuses rehearsed. By the way, how is the daughter?"

"She's doing okay. She and a young deputy have developed a relationship, so at least that's promising."

We talked for a few more minutes about a problem she was having with an employee. A vet's assistant interrupted our conversation by waving me to come to her. I did, and she walked me back to a small office where one of the veterinarians sat on a chair. He stood when I entered and motioned me to sit in the second chair.

"Chubbs has an intestinal blockage. You haven't noticed anything before today?"

"No, but tell me, is he going to be okay?"

"We'll need to keep him overnight, maybe two nights, but he should be fine. I don't believe he'll need surgery, but the procedure we'll have to perform isn't a pleasant one. If everything goes well, he'll be like new in a day or two. If we need to do surgery, do you want us to call you first?"

"No, do what you have to do."

"Okay, we'll have some forms for you to sign. He's not a young dog, but he should handle the surgery just fine."

I signed the forms but had a hard time focusing on the words. Chubbs had been with me ever since I moved back to Clovis. I kept telling myself it would be a simple procedure, and he would be home tomorrow. I left, forgetting to look around to see if Nancy was still there.

Chapter 20

Carlos and Vic headed north on New Mexico state highway 330 in the white van. The sun had set, but darkness had not yet chased away the last remnants of daylight. Carlos drove the van through a highway construction zone ignoring the temporary lower speed limit. Within seconds, a state trooper's vehicle whipped in behind them with flashers on.

"Damn," Carlos muttered.

Vic saw him looking in his rear-view mirror and turned around. "Pull over. Maybe he'll just give us a warning."

Carlos did. They both knew the van wouldn't flag anything in the trooper's data base. The van was registered to the company, and Lara's name was the only name now publicly associated with it.

The state trooper parked a good ten yards behind them. He didn't immediately get out of the car.

"Did you see anyone working back there?" Carlos asked.

"No, did you?" Vic said.

"No. I thought the speed limit only applied if workers were present."

"We'll see."

Gus Travers, the state trooper, climbed out of his car and stretched before ambling toward the van. His indigestion bothered him, and the anger that developed from his spat with his boss still lingered.

"Stay in the vehicle. I need your license and the registration."

"What for? We didn't do anything wrong."

"Just hand them over. What's in the van?"

"We're empty," Carlos said.

Vic opened the glove compartment and reached for the registration, momentarily forgetting that he had placed a pistol in the glove box before they left Roswell.

Experience and training had taught Travers to keep a good eye on the contents of a glove box whenever anyone reached into it for the registration. He saw the pistol.

"Stop right there!" Travers shouted and pulled his service weapon from his holster.

Before he could get in a position to use his weapon, Carlos pulled a small .38 caliber revolver from under the dash and shot him twice point blank into his chest. Travers stepped backwards before collapsing onto the pavement.

"Quick we have to move fast," Carlos said. He jumped out of the van, and Vic did the same.

The two picked Travers up and carried him back to his car. They put him in the passenger seat, and Vic hustled around to the driver's side.

"Over there," Vic said, pointing to a small mound a hundred or so yards off their side of the road. "Follow me."

Vic drove off the road and sped through the flat terrain ignoring any holes and small bushes in his way. Carlos followed in the van, but he drove with more caution not wanting to mess up the van's suspension or blow a tire. They both parked behind the mound making them almost invisible to any passing traffic.

"We got a break that no traffic passed us back there," Carlos said.

"There's never much traffic on that road. We need to destroy the cameras and the data."

"You also left your DNA in there. We best burn the whole car."

"How do you recommend we do that?" Vic asked.

They decided to syphon gas out of their van and pour it over Travers and the inside of his vehicle. They put an extra dose on the console with the computer and opened the cap to the gas tank. After letting three cars go by and not seeing any vehicles in either direction, they lit the state car on fire and drove back to the highway in the van. They turned south. The trooper's vehicle exploded a few seconds after Vic and Carlos started driving towards Roswell.

They took the first side road they reached. The forty-five minute drive turned into a two hour one, but it kept them safe from any check points or road blocks. They would have to wait a while longer to return to Melrose and make their final effort to find the necklace.

Gus Travers never had a chance to learn that he did not die in vain. His death allowed a nearly nineteen-year-old young woman in Melrose to live through the night.

Chapter 21

"Come on Chubbs, let's go home," I said the next morning as I walked him out of the vet's office and to my car. The assistant who had been so concerned with the spelling of his name told me that surgery hadn't been necessary. She said Chubbs would be tired for the rest of the day, but should otherwise be good as new. She also suggested I keep him on dog food and stay away from letting him eat my leftovers.

"I wonder where she got the idea I ever had left overs." Chubbs looked up at me from the passenger seat. "So, what do you think? Stick with dog food or continue cooking for two?" I reached over and scratched his neck, and he licked my hand. "I agree, but I guess we could both use smaller portions."

The next few days passed uneventfully. Chubbs seemed to be doing fine, and I finished the section of the cinder block fence. Josh completed his class and had all but moved in with Jessie. I talked to Jessie on the phone once, and she seemed happy.

The Friday late morning phone call from Mickie broke up the lull in the action.

"Jim, I need you to come see me this morning. Can you do that?"

No hello, how are you doing, but at least she asked me to come see her this time. "Of course, what's up?"

"I'll tell you when you get here. How soon?"

"I'll come out now. I have something to do later this afternoon."

"Good. I'll be waiting for you."

I drove to her property, wondering if I should have asked her to come to me. I dismissed that thought. I knew she didn't go anywhere unless she had to.

As before, she stood on the front porch with her dogs and watched my arrival. I nodded when I got out of my car.

"Come on in. We need to talk." She led me into the dining room. We sat in the same seats we used before. "How much do you know about what's been happening?" she asked.

"With regard to the investigation?"

"Is there anything else we've been talking about?" She didn't try to hide the sarcasm in her voice.

"No, but I've heard nothing since the last time we talked. We talked about Cobb's disappearance, right?"

"As deep as you are into all this, I'm surprised they've stopped talking to you. No, I guess I shouldn't be."

"What's happened?"

"A hell of a lot. A couple days ago, they found Cobb in a shed behind an abandoned house. The house was less than a mile off highway 330. The night before last, someone killed a state trooper on the same highway about fifty miles north of Roswell. I don't like coincidences. I especially don't like them when they result in two killings near the same remote highway and within a few days of each other. By the way, that's the road someone would take to Melrose if you came up from the south. Do you know how many murder victims were found along that section of the road in the last decade? Zero."

"You've got good sources."

"Better than you obviously. It's more than just good sources. I have a friend, who came out of Afghanistan in lot worse shape than me, who has dedicated his life to, let's say, analytics for a couple big national agencies. He's my mole," she said and smiled. "I have other contacts who have given me the basics we discussed before. This friend is putting everything into his computer that does all this analyzing stuff. I hope I'm being sufficiently vague."

"You are, plus I have a poor memory."

"Good. I need you to know this, but don't breathe a word of it to anyone. Understand?"

"Yes."

"If you do, I'll feed whatever is left of your manhood to my dogs." She grinned, but I couldn't tell if she was just joking or was thinking how much she might like to do just that.

"Mickie, come on. You don't need to threaten me."

"I know, but there are a group of us that need to be left alone. We've earned that. Anyway, what I was getting to is that he believes this recent killing of the state trooper is directly involved. The same killers, he thinks there are two, are involved. The timing, the location, the FBI's belief that a pair of hired guns live in the Roswell area--"

"They know that?" I said, interrupting her.

"As you might expect, the FBI has quite a database on organized crime. They're quite good at tweaking it. Not good enough at coming up with individuals' names yet, or pulling actionable evidence out of the ether, but excellent in other ways."

"And they're telling you this?"

"Heavens, no. My friend has the access, and he knows I'm very interested."

"How do I fit into this?"

"Convince Josh to either move in with Jessie or bring her to his place. Talk to your contacts with the sheriff's office to get more patrols out there. Spend more time out there yourself. You don't have to be at her house. Find a spot where you can surveil the house without being obvious."

"Your friend thinks they're coming back?"

"Not just my friend, the FBI does, too. If we're lucky you may run into an FBI surveillance team in the area. They should have one out there, but as usual they're stretched thin, so it's unlikely."

"Why don't you take some of your things and stay at her house. She likes you," I said.

"You know I can't."

I didn't know that but kept any comment to myself.

"Do your sources have any timeline for the killers returning to Melrose?"

"The theory he passed along to me was that they were heading that way when they were stopped by the now dead state trooper. It's only a theory, but it fits. No one has any other explanation."

"Wasn't there any data from the vehicle, you know, like camera footage?"

"Camera footage? How old are you? But no, not yet. The vehicle was burned to a crisp. The forensics people are trying to piece things together."

"But they're sure it wasn't an accident?"

"The guy was burned bad enough to kill him but not bad enough to melt the two rounds in his chest. Everyone hopes that shots killed him before he was set on fire."

"Me, too. Your source can't push the FBI a little?"

"No. This is our battle," she said.

"It's not really a fair fight, is it?"

"Didn't they teach you when it comes to fighting, I mean

really fighting, you can't let fair get in the way."

"I know." I did, too. Not in the way she did. Mickie's military experience put her at the tip of the spear. Mine had its scary moments but nothing comparable to hers. In fact, due to some ironic twist of fate, I had learned more about "kill or be killed" after I retired from the military.

"I give them thirty days, at the most, more likely a couple of weeks."

"Until they return?"

"Yes," she said. "They have no reason to wait any longer."

"If I was rich like you, I'd send her on a lengthy vacation to get her out of the area."

"I'm not rich. Besides the more I think about it, the more I'm convinced the only solution is eliminating the threat. Even if they search the house and don't find anything, they'll continue to have a nagging question. Could she tell them what she did with it?"

"That's a stretch."

"These people aren't rational. How could they be? I'm toying with the thought that it could be a man and a woman team doing this."

"Any reason?"

"No, none at all."

"How do you propose we get rid of the threat?"

"Ideally, the authorities will get the job done. Otherwise, you and Josh may be stuck doing it. And Jessie, of course."

"Let's hope it doesn't come to that. I'll be seeing Jessie later this afternoon."

"Her birthday party?"

"Yes, are you going to be there?" I asked.

"She called me and told me about it. She hinted around about my coming, but I made it clear to her that I couldn't. I asked her not to tell anyone about me either. I know she's mentioned me to Josh."

"He knows to be quiet about you."

"You talked to him about me?"

"After he already knew about you and Jessie. I told him not to talk about you with anyone else. I don't think he will."

"Thanks. In case you don't know, her aunt will try to get you to stay there after everyone leaves. I thought I should warn you."

"Why does everyone think they have to warn me?"

"The fact that they do pretty much answers that question. Don't you think? I have to admit, I'm hoping you do spend the night. Jessie's aunt will spill the beans to Jessie and probably half the city. But don't worry, I'm sure Jessie will pass on all the gory details to me, and I'll let you know what everyone's saying."

"Thanks," I said and frowned. I had no intention of staying long at the party. Once the presents were opened, I planned to find some excuse to leave.

We talked for another five minutes about the threat to Jessie. We had no solutions. As we walked out to my car, she grabbed my right elbow with her left hand. She stared at me with her serious look.

"I know you don't like carrying a weapon around. It's a stupid attitude. You draw mayhem wherever you go. What good are you going to be to Jessie out there without a weapon if these two killers show up? You can't reason with them. You'll end up dead and be no help to anyone. If you go out there, take your Beretta. Do you hear me, Jim?"

"Yes."

She let go of me, and I left.

Chapter 22

When I arrived home, I checked up on Chubbs before I did anything else. I found him curled up on my bed asleep. He was breathing normally, and the fact that he had jumped up onto the bed indicated to me that he was feeling better. I left him alone and went to the kitchen to grab a beer. I had a lot to think about.

I knew Mickie was right about taking my Beretta with me when I went out to Jessie's. Her theory about the killers returning also made sense. It didn't irritate me that Deputy Johnny Willis hadn't passed on as much information to me as Mickie had. I knew there was a good possibility the FBI hadn't shared the information yet with the locals.

Now that a state trooper had been killed the state would undoubtedly raise the resources they had dedicated to catch the killers. That was to our advantage, but I also knew after a week or so the intense effort would be scaled back.

I thought about trying to find something to watch on television but the remote was out of reach. My beer and the recliner I occupied overruled my thoughts of doing anything, so I closed my eyes to think.

Chubbs woke me up an hour later with a soft bark. I glanced around and saw him at the sliding door to the backyard. I stood up and let him out. He moved around the yard as though nothing had happened to him in the last two days. That lifted my spirits. My phone rang, disrupting my mood.

"Jim, this is Josh. You are coming to the party this afternoon, aren't you?"

"Yes. I may not be there when it starts, but I'll be there by six. Why? What's up?"

"Nothing, Jessie is just getting antsy. There aren't too many invited, so she wanted me to make sure you'd be there."

I felt like asking "Jessie or her aunt?" but didn't. "How are things going in the investigation?"

"Nothing new. I'm not sure if that's good or bad. Oh, one thing, they found Mr. Cobb's body. Someone beat him to death and hid his body in an abandoned shed."

"That's too bad."

"We think it's related but can't prove anything. He wasn't found in our county. Hopefully, his death will be an end to all this killing."

"That would be nice, but I doubt if it's over," I said. "By the way, I bought Jessie a gift card. Think that's okay."

"That's perfect. I did the same thing. Gotta go, I'll see you soon."

After the call, I wondered if anyone bought personal gifts anymore. It seemed like the consensus around here was that one doesn't. I felt like telling Josh that gold and diamonds were the way to a lady's heart, not a plastic gift card. Plastic? Boy, was I falling further behind. Everything was digital now.

My phone rang again. Normally, I receive two or three calls a week. I thought this week might set a record. Looking at caller ID made me smile.

"Hey, Rose, how are you doing?" FBI Special Agent Rose Luna and I had a special arrangement. Unfortunately, she lived on the east coast, and I spent my days in New Mexico. Over the past two plus years, we had managed by purpose or fate to spend some time together. I enjoyed those times, despite both of us being shot, stabbed, and assaulted in other ways. I believed she did, too.

"Good. I'm sitting still in this damn traffic. Something must have happened on the bridge. Anyway, I thought while I waited, I'd give you a call. I miss you."

"Miss you, too. How's work?"

"Not much going on lately. How about you? Staying out of trouble?"

"Actually not. Want to hear about it?"

"Absolutely," she said.

I summarized what was going on with Jessie and my involvement in it. She listened with only a few interruptions for me to clarify a point. "Poor girl, she must be terrified."

"I don't think she fully appreciates the situation, but she is frightened. I don't think anyone here wants to scare her more than they need to."

"What are you doing?"

"Trying to ensure she gets as much on-scene police protection as possible. I see her now and then. Can you believe I'm going to her birthday party in a few minutes?"

"A birthday party?"

"Yes, long story, I'd rather not be going."

"Go and have fun. She must really like you to invite you to her party."

"More like her aunt invited me."

"Well, good for you. There are no chains on you, you know," she said.

"Rose, her aunt is not my style. I'm only going to be polite."

"Want me to dig around and see what's going on at our end with this Mario Pascual guy?"

"Only if you can do it without irritating someone. We're thinking whoever these killers are they will make one more attempt to find the necklace by going through Jessie. That is what we cannot allow."

"Want me to take a few days off and come out there?"

"Thanks for the offer, and while I'd love to see you, I'd rather you stick with our plan to spend a week in Colorado in June. I'd hate to mess that up."

"Okay, that would be more fun. Just don't get yourself shot or something and make us miss the trip," she said.

"I won't." We talked for another five minutes about a problem she was having with the plumbing at her apartment. When her traffic started moving, we ended the call.

Rose's comments about having no chains tying me down bothered me. We had agreed to it, and we knew it was the only way to handle our relationship. I believed we had a goal that down the road when she was ready to retire or just walk away from the job, we would end up together. Our lives had taken us in two different directions. When we were together, the chemistry and attraction was real. However, her life had too many moving parts with a new career with the FBI and a desire to prove herself. My life? Well, my life had me firmly stuck in a rut. Ironically, for reasons I couldn't explain, I had no desire at the moment to extricate myself from that rut.

I let Chubbs inside, and he promptly went to his food bowl. I smiled at how much we were alike.

Chapter 23

Carlos and Vic sipped on their drinks and watched the dancer on the pole in front of them. The bar could hardly be called upper class, but both men would be way out of place in an upper-class cocktail lounge. They knew it and didn't care.

"I could stay here forever," Vic said as the dancer gave him a suggestive smile. "You know, she has three sisters."

"You keep saying that, and I keep telling you no way. I've seen those sisters. They definitely come from a different gene pool. Drink up, it's after midnight."

Vic tilted his whiskey glass back and swallowed the remaining ounce or two. The ice in the glass crashed against his upper lip and spilled over the side. Carlos' glass was already empty. The basket of chips in front of them had been empty for some time.

"This is truly bad whiskey. Why do I order it every night?" Vic asked.

"Because it's the only whiskey they have. You should be drinking tequila, like me. My brother, you got no respect for your heritage. Let's go. She knows how to get to your room." Carlos motioned with his head at the dancer.

The two rose from the table. Carlos headed for the door while Vic moved closer to the dance floor and talked briefly with the woman. Carlos didn't remember the woman's name. Vic turned away from the woman and walked toward him with a big, stupid grin on his face.

"Come on, man, we're not in high school. You act like she just agreed to go steady."

"I'm in love."

Carlos chose to ignore Vic's remark. The mixture of alcohol and women brought out this side of him.

Carlos thought the two of them had been pretty smart since killing the state trooper. They had returned to Roswell and stayed long enough to trade out the license tag with another identical white van that was down for maintenance. They then left Roswell for Alamogordo and checked into a hotel.

"You know, we need to finish this," Carlos said.

"I know, but not tonight. I've got plans for tonight."

"Yeah, well, you have a nice night, but tomorrow you need to sleep. I can't be hauling your ass to Melrose and do everything for you because you can't stay awake."

"She's an animal," Vic shook his head. "I think she must take something before she gets to my room, because she wears me out."

"I'm not interested, but this is the last night. Okay? You can always come back on your own after we're done."

"Sure, no problem."

Carlos knew there wouldn't be one. They had already been in Alamogordo for eight days. Lara had told them nothing irregular had happened at the office or with the company since they left. He had seen a couple short news updates regarding the death of the state trooper on the television, but the updates simply reported there was nothing new to report.

They had spent a couple days in the small city evaluating the possibility of opening a branch office for their employment location service they had in Roswell. They found two small independent companies, but one looked like it may have closed.

He and Vic had a dream of someday retiring from their world of crime and living off the income stream from their legitimate business. To do that and live comfortably, though, they would have to expand their business.

Carlos woke up at eight in the morning and walked to the Denny's across the street. He didn't bother Vic. If the woman had come to his room, he imagined they'd both stay in bed until noon. He ordered eggs, bacon and toast and chased it down with two cups of coffee. The server took his order and brought him his breakfast, but she didn't linger and talk.

Ever since high school, which he never finished, Carlos wanted to have that tough guy look. Nature had already done a lot of the work. His dark hair, somewhat pointed nose and narrow eyes accompanied a mouth that had a natural scowl. He rarely smiled. He had perfected the ability to stare at you without blinking. One could almost see the daggers coming out of those dark eyes. While he had started working out as a teenager, the level and intensity of those workouts increased ten-fold while he served his time in prison. The tight, black tee shirt he wore accentuated the weight-lifter-look. He stood a half inch under six feet but his boots added that back in.

The downside of his "look" came as an unspoken challenge to other tough guys. It didn't happen often, as even tough guys realize that getting into a fight for no reason is usually not an intelligent thing to do. Prison fights aside, Carlos had encountered a half dozen men over the past fifteen years who had some internal need to prove themselves. Each of these events happened at a bar or some other venue where his attacker had consumed enough alcohol to mess with his common sense. If his assailant had any common sense to begin with, that is.

One of these fights ended in a draw. The two men beat themselves to the point where they eventually stopped fighting, and someone pulled them away from each other. One of the fights Carlos could barely remember. He had lost that one badly. All the others ended badly for the other person. Vic had the job of patching Carlos up as needed or, in the one he lost, taking him to a hospital.

At first glance, one might think Vic was a happy-go-lucky type of a guy. Carlos' opposite. Vic's lighter brown hair, rounder face, thinner features, and natural grin put people at ease. For the most part, that would be the correct reaction. However, Vic had a crazy, cruel streak that hid behind that wholesome veneer. He kept that cruel streak under tight control, but when he unleashed it, look out. Carlos often told Vic that he had only two true loves: women and his machete.

Vic liked to think of himself as a lover, not a fighter. To the common observer, he could easily fit into that category. Those who knew him well, though, weren't fooled. When Vic flipped that switch, he could become quite terrifying, and even Carlos could never be too sure when that moment could come. Vic had told him that he had control over that switch, that it wasn't a simple reflex, but Carlos often wondered about that.

Carlos considered Vic more dangerous than himself. Carlos didn't look for fights and would make an effort to avoid them; however, he could only be pushed so far. Once he walked away from a confrontation, he put the matter behind him.

Vic, on the other hand, would take a lot of humiliation to avoid a fight, but he didn't let it go. Later, he would ambush the individual, using a rock, brick, or other weapon. He only brought out his machete if he intended on killing someone.

The two men, ruthless killers each, somehow got along. Both considered the other to be a true brother and the only family they had left.

"I thought I'd find you here," Vic said as he approached the table.

Carlos had watched Vic walk across the street to the restaurant. "I'm surprised you're awake this early."

"Her mom called about twenty minutes ago. She said she needed her to come home. Her mom cut her hand or something." Vic sat down and waved at the server. He gave her a big smile.

"Good morning, would you like to order something?" she said and returned the smile.

"I'll have what my friend here is having."

"Coffee, too?"

"Please, and put everything on my bill. My grumpy friend is a lousy tipper." Vic winked at her.

Carlos shook his head as the server walked away. She had not made eye contact with him. "Did you tell your friend you were leaving today?"

"Of course. She knows we're here on a business trip. She said she would wait for me."

"Don't tell me you believe her."

Vic smiled but didn't answer. "Have you decided whether we are going all the way tonight, or are we going to spend the night back home?"

"I think your recommendation to stay in Roswell tonight is a good one. It's Saturday, and we can hit the club and be seen. Tomorrow we can watch the game with some of the guys. Then we can head north just after the game. We can be back by breakfast."

"No one will know we left town. Besides, you need a night with Carmen. You're too uptight," Vic said.

"You know, it's going to piss me off if we don't find that necklace. We can't kill the girl until we're absolutely sure, okay?"

"Don't worry, we can take our time with her. If it's not there, that's just the way it is. I bet it never got this far, anyway."

"I imagine you're right. Let's hope they pay us something for our time," Carlos said.

"They will. They always do. I'm more concerned they might think we found it and kept it. That would not be good."

"Don't go there. They would have to go through a lot of bodies before they would ever get to us, and the deal is that they aren't told who we are."

"Yeah, that's the way it's supposed to be. Let's hope it really is."

Chapter 24

I parked on the street in front Vicky Perez' house. The driveway already had a black pickup truck and Jessie's motorcycle on it. Someone had parked a blue Toyota on the street directly in front of the house. Another guest, I thought.

The front door to the house opened before I reached it, and Vicky stepped out. She must have been watching for me. "Jim, Jim, come in. Jessie was worried you might not come."

"I'm here." I doubted that Jessie was very worried.

She surprised me with a hug when I reached the doorway. "We'll have a good time tonight. It'll be the three kids and us. We can break away after the cake."

I wouldn't refer to Josh as a kid, but I imagined he was one of the three. I also doubted that she meant I could leave when she said we could break away after the cake.

Vicky rested her hand on my elbow as she walked me into the house. "We have beer. I understand you're a beer drinker."

"Sure," I said and wondered how and where she had learned that about me.

"Jessie, Jim is here. Please bring him a beer," she shouted.

Jessie stepped out of the kitchen. "Hi, Jim, I didn't hear the doorbell. One cold beer coming up."

Josh walked out of the kitchen as Jessie went back in. "Hi, Jim. Glad you could make it. I didn't want to be the only male here."

I nodded in understanding. Another teenager, a female, walked out of the kitchen and stopped next to Josh. I saw her bump her hand against Josh's arm. He looked at her, and she motioned with her eyes toward me.

"Jim this is Yvette. She's a good friend of Jessie's. And me, now," Josh said with a smile. Yvette smiled back at him.

"Hi, Yvette, nice to meet you."

"You, too," she said. Yvette put her right hand on her hip and posed. I thought it was something she had perfected over the years. Like she was saying look at me, aren't I pretty. I didn't think she needed the pose, but it worked. She was very pretty. No, pretty didn't really cover it. She had a look that pulled on me. Captivating might be a better word. I had a hard time looking away.

"Yvette," Jessie called from the kitchen. Yvette went to her. She returned a second later and brought me a can of Coors beer.

"Has Jessie finished with the enchiladas?" Vicky asked.

"Just about. She asked me to ask you to come help her for a second," Josh said.

After the two left, Josh and I sat down on opposite ends of the couch.

"What's with Yvette? I saw her pinch your arm as she and Vicky went by."

"Oh man, I don't know what's going on. She's been touching me a lot. I only met her yesterday. I can't tell you how mixed up my mind is right now."

"She's a pretty girl."

"So is Jessie," Josh said.

"Doesn't she know you and Jessie are kind of an item?"

"I don't know what she knows. And I'm not sure what Jessie and I are."

"Well, one thing you are is her bodyguard. Unofficially, I

know, but we both know she is not out of danger yet. So, you need to put any ideas of spending much time with Yvette off for a while."

"No, I know that. I'm not going to abandon Jessie. I really like her, too. It's just every time Yvette gets close, my emotions go crazy. You know what I mean."

"I do. What has Jessie told you about her?"

"They've been friends since grade school. She warned me about her, too. Apparently, she has a reputation, but Jessie doesn't let that interfere with their friendship. They've both been through some hard times."

"I'm no expert and certainly shouldn't be giving advice, but I imagine it's normal for any guy to get a little flustered when someone like Yvette rubs up against them. You just need to remember this is no time to start paying less attention to Jessie."

"You think the killer is coming back, don't you?"

"I think the next two to three weeks are critical," I said.

"You should come out to the house Sunday. I've finished up with the security system and new locks. I'm sure Jessie won't mind. She gets done with the horses by four, but I'm not sure if she's working on Sunday."

"Are you staying out there?"

Josh blushed and smiled. "Not all the time."

"Check with Jessie and let me know what time to be out there."

"Great. Maybe I'll grill some steaks."

Vicky stepped out of the kitchen. "Come on, it's time to get the party started." She led us through the kitchen to the small dining room. Three colorful balloons were floating in the air. Jessie pushed them toward the wall and away from the table.

Someone had filled the balloons with helium and tied small weights to them with a ribbon that let the weights hang about a foot below the balloon. The balloons were all alike and had Happy Birthday written across them.

Decorative paper plates and napkins, each inscribed with Happy Birthday, had been placed on the round table in front of five chairs. The table looked like it could handle six chairs, but I didn't see another chair in the room.

"You're here," Vicky said and pulled out a chair for me.

"Thanks," I said and stood behind it.

"Yvette, you're here next to me," Vicky said and pointed to a chair two over from me. "And then Jess and Josh."

Everyone obediently moved to their seats. I would be sitting between Vicky and Josh. A long, narrow rectangular table ran half the length of the wall off to my right. Our dinner had been placed on it in a mix of baskets and trays.

"Please sit, everyone," Vicky said. Jessie and Yvette giggled about something while Josh and I sat down. Vicky moved two baskets of tortilla chips and two small bowls of salsa from the side table and placed them in front of us.

"Do you like enchiladas, Jim?" she asked.

"I sure do."

"Good. I knew everyone else did." Carrying a silver platter, she leaned against me and scooped a couple enchiladas out of the platter and placed them on my plate. She repeated the process, but I noted she didn't seem to need to lean against anyone else while she served them the enchiladas.

She repeated the process bringing refried beans and then rice to the table. Finally, she placed a basket of flour tortillas in the middle of the table.

"Eat up," she instructed. No one hesitated.

"These are delicious," Josh said, and Jessie nodded in agreement.

"I use the same recipe my mother did," Vicky said, holding up a forkful of enchilada. "Jessie can make them, too."

"They are very good," I said.

"Thank you, Jim."

I suddenly felt her hand squeeze my thigh.

After we finished dinner, I thought there would be a period where gifts would be given to Jessie, but there wasn't. We went straight to the cake and singing Happy Birthday. Yvette complimented Vicky on the angel food birthday cake, and everyone else expressed their agreement. Josh and I had second pieces.

Vicky stood up and grabbed some plates and headed into the kitchen. Jessie and Yvette followed her, each carrying empty plates and silverware.

"When do we give the presents to Jessie?" I asked Josh.

"Oh, I gave mine to her this morning. Her aunt gave her something when we arrived. I don't think Yvette got her anything."

"I have a gift card for her."

"Jessie, come here for a minute," Josh called out without warning.

She did, and Josh told her I had something for her.

Awkward, I thought. I stood and fumbled in my pocket for the paper I printed the gift card on. "I didn't know what to get for you. I hope you can use this."

She took the piece of paper and studied it. For a second, I thought she didn't know what it was, but then she smiled and gave me a hug. "You printed it out. That's good, now I can keep this with my journals. Look what Josh gave me." She pulled a necklace out from the front of her blouse.

"That's nice," I said. The necklace held a small silver horse with a diamond on the side of a saddle. So much for his comment about a gift card, I thought.

She beamed, and Josh smiled and blushed. "He's so sweet," she said. She hugged him and they kissed. I made my way into the kitchen where Vicky and Yvette were just leaving to go into the backyard. I followed them and was surprised to find a small in-ground pool. A table with four chairs sat off to one side of the pool on the concrete patio. Vicky sat at the table and motioned me to join her. The evening darkness had settled in, but I could still see the remnants of a red sky off to the west.

"I think everything went very well tonight," I said.

"Thanks, Jim. I hope Jessie had a nice time."

"She did," Yvette said. "You know, if we had more privacy Aunt Vicky, I would go skinny dipping right now."

"You can," Vicky said and winked at me.

"No, not tonight, Jessie would kill me, but it would be fun. You wouldn't mind, would you, Jim?" Her eyes seemed to twinkle in the semi-darkness.

"Not at all."

"Ha! Next time," she said and walked back inside.

"I sometimes think she, rather than Jessie, must be my sister's child. Maybe that's why Jessie likes her. Reminds her of her mom. Yvette is as nice as she can be, but she's a wild one."

"I can see that. She called you Aunt Vicky, too."

"I've known her since she was a baby. Melrose is a tiny town. She and Jessie have been like sisters since before kindergarten.

You know, if Josh wasn't here, she would've had no problem with stripping down and jumping into the pool."

"She said Jessie would kill her."

"That's because Josh is here. Yvette would love to tease the poor young man and drive him crazy, but I don't think she would do anything to hurt Jessie."

"We're going to head out," Jessie said from the backdoor. I could see Josh standing behind her. "Josh is driving us back to Melrose."

Vicky stood up and walked toward them. "Take the cake with you."

"Already have it. Thanks!"

They closed the door. Vicky and I talked for another fifteen minutes about Anita and what happened to her. She had learned a little more from the police but still had questions. I tried to answer most of them.

"I need to head home, Vicky. It's been a nice evening," I said when the conversation started to dwindle.

"I was hoping you could stay. We could swim a little and you know."

"I didn't think to bring my swimsuit."

"You don't need one. It gets quite dark here and the neighbors don't have a good angle to see anyway."

"My dog had an operation yesterday. I need to get home to check on him and give him his medicine."

"Oh, wish you could stay, but I understand. You're welcome to come back anytime," she said.

"I appreciate that, Vicky."

We both stood and walked through the house to the front yard. She stopped by the door, and I continued to my car. On the way home, I felt a little relieved, but at the same time, the little devil in the back of my mind was calling me an idiot for not taking advantage of the situation.

Chapter 25

Chubbs greeted me at the door to the garage. I led him to the front and stayed with him while he did his usual checks.

"It looks like you've fully recovered from your visit to the vet. You know you gave me a scare there," I said. He ignored me and continued sniffing along the front of the house for another minute. The half dozen holly bushes that line part of the front wall give him plenty of places to sniff. When I opened the door to go inside, he bounded over to me.

"Come on," I said, and we both went inside.

As I was getting into bed my phone buzzed. I checked it and discovered a text from Josh. "We both want you to come to Jessie's, but can you come late afternoon or maybe around six."

I texted him back saying late afternoon was fine and received a thumbs-up emoji back. I was tempted to ask him if he would be spending the night with her but decided not to. My interest focused on her safety, but I imagined my question could be received as not being my business.

The next day, I didn't do much but work around the yard and read a book. Chubbs supervised my yard work, but seemed more content resting on his pillow in the house while I read.

My phone rang Sunday morning and woke me from a sound sleep. Daylight peeked through the blinds. Chubbs looked up at me with what I figured was an annoyed expression.

"Hello," I said without checking caller ID.

"Did I wake you?" I easily recognized Mickie's voice.

"Yes, what time is it?"

"Seven, you should be awake by now. We need to talk again, and you need to practice more. When can you get out here?"

"Give me an hour. Do you have coffee?"

"No," she said and ended the call.

I felt like making it two hours. She didn't need to be so gruff, but I knew Mickie wasn't one to waste time. It had only been forty-eight hours since I was last there. Something important must have developed.

After letting Chubbs outside, I made a cup of coffee and a bowl of Cheerios for my breakfast. The only topic in which Mickie and I shared an interest was Jessie, so my curiosity was piqued. I hadn't heard anything in the past week from the sheriff's office. Even Josh had nothing new to tell me at the party.

Mickie was waiting for me on her front porch when I drove down her driveway. Her two dogs sat next to her. She stayed seated on the wooden rocker as I stepped out of the Mustang. She had a red cup in her left hand and took a sip. The dogs stared at me like I was a jackrabbit, and I imagined they were waiting for the attack command.

"Did you bring your Berretta?"

"Yes," I moved my right hand to the left side of my chest.

"Good. It's well concealed. Come on in. We have a problem."

"We?"

"Don't be a smart ass," she said and stood. "Come on." She wore matching khaki slacks and shirt.

"Looks like you're going on a safari."

"I wish." Mickie led me to the dining room. "Sit down. You drink your coffee black, right?"

"Yes. Now you have me worried," I said, thinking she had

never offered me anything before and had told me she didn't have any.

"Don't get used to it." She disappeared for a minute before returning with a plain white cup in her hand. She set it on the table in front of me before sitting on the chair across from me. A set of ear protectors sat on the table in front of each of us.

"Thanks."

"The FBI is losing interest in our case."

"Already? We just talked. Do they think the threat is gone?"

"No, of course not. It's a matter of priorities. The regional office out here is still working with the state police, but all extra resources have been pulled back. The state and county still have it listed as a top priority, but the bust last night of a truckload of illegals near Santa Fe has pulled away a lot of their resources, too."

"I heard about that. They arrested two traffickers, and discovered some thirty people crammed in the trailer."

"Yes. Traffickers, low life scum. They should shoot them all."

"Have you gotten any impression that they think the threat to Jessie has diminished? It's been what, several days since Cobb was found."

"No, and I answered that already. Pay attention. The passage of time always undermines one's vigilance."

I felt like this was how she lectured to a bunch of army trainees. "And that's what is happening here," I said. "I get it. It makes as much sense that the bad guys are keeping a low profile rather than giving up entirely."

"Bingo. I had another long discussion with my contact on this. He runs everything through his computer to find the odds, etc. He loves this new AI crap. He thinks the next two weeks will be the critical window, and he believes they will certainly return to make one more attempt to find the necklace. They will kill her in the process. They won't wait for the house to be empty. They'll want to find out if she knows anything about it."

I nodded. "So, hiding her for a few weeks may not help."

"No, in their mind, they need to interrogate her."

"If they killed the state trooper, and our bet is they did, then Josh's presence won't cause them to turn around and go home."

"Right. They will come prepared to kill anyone who is in their way. That means you, too, if you're there," she said.

"But you still want me there," I said and grinned.

"We need you there. You don't die so easily."

"One more body to go through." I said, half joking.

"You got it," she said. Her cold blue eyes stared into mine.

"It'd be nice if you came along with me."

"I can't leave here."

I doubted that very much, but I knew arguing with her would be a waste of time.

"By the way, how was the party last night?" she asked.

"It was fine. I think Jessie had a good time." I didn't correct her reference to last night.

"And you? Did you score with the aunt?"

"You sure you weren't in the Marines? You have no manners," I said.

"So, is that a yes?"

"No."

"Damn, I didn't think so. You're too uptight. You overthink things."

"Can we go outside now. I'd like to get some practice in." I didn't need her lectures, and despite my determination to never allow her to get underneath my skin, she was starting to do just that.

"Come on," she said. She grabbed an ear protector. I did the same and followed her.

On the way out, she grabbed a rifle that leaned against the wall by the back door. She carried it in one hand and seemed very comfortable with it. Although I'm no expert at identifying rifles, this one looked like a large hunting rifle. A sniper rifle, I thought.

"Use that in the Army?"

"When I had to. Not the one I usually carried."

I remained silent, thinking she might say something more, but she didn't. We stopped about ten yards in front of the bench. Twelve diet coke cans had already been placed on the bench in a line, about four inches apart.

"When you're ready, I want you to hit all the cans in ten seconds. Take as many shots as you need. You do have enough rounds in your Beretta?"

"I do." Once before I didn't, and she reprimanded me, saying only a fool carries a half- loaded gun.

"The trick is to not think, just do. See each can first, then squeeze the trigger. Don't do it the other way around."

I reached for my Beretta and aimed at the first can.

"Whenever you're ready."

I fired, and the first can went flying off the bench. I hit three in a row before I missed the fourth. I fired again at it and hit it. I hit the next four in succession.

"Cease fire," she shouted.

I re-holstered and moved my ear protectors to around my neck.

"Not bad for an old man. Accuracy is more important than

speed, but speed is relevant. The guy trying to kill you won't give you any extra time. Nor will his buddies."

"I know. Hitting all twelve cans in ten seconds is nearly impossible."

"It's not. You took time to watch each can fly off the bench. That was your only fault. Next time don't watch the cans. Shoot and immediately move to the next can. Don't get distracted."

I reloaded and repeated the drill. It only took two more efforts for me to hit ten of the twelve cans in the ten seconds. On my fourth attempt, I again hit ten cans.

"That's enough, you have the idea," she said.

"Can you do it?" I asked, knowing she could. I wanted to see her do it.

She looked at me for a minute, probably wondering if I was worth the effort. "Load it and give it to me." At least she didn't order me to replace the cans this time. She did that while I reloaded. She took the pistol and held it down by her side.

"Say when."

"Don't you want to put a round in the chamber?"

"Say when."

"When."

In one fluid motion, Mickie raised her arm, placed her left foot forward, pulled the slide back and let it slam forward, putting a round in the chamber, and fired off twelve rounds. The cans all went flying. She handed the weapon back to me.

"How long?"

"I forgot to count," I said.

She laughed. "I actually like showing off. I tell you what, clean up the brass, and I'll do the cans later. I want to see if this old thing works." She walked a few yards off to the right and picked up the rifle from the ground where she had placed it.

I picked up the brass and dropped them in a plastic coffee can that she left there for that purpose. When I turned around, she was arranging a mat on the ground. I looked down range and, in the distance, saw a post with what looked like a paper plate fixed to it.

"Are you going to try to hit that white plate or whatever it is?"

She glanced at me but didn't say anything. I looked again at the target in the distance. The post that held the target was farther out than I had ever seen one before. "That's three hundred yards, right?"

She placed the rifle on the mat, slid on her ear protectors, and awkwardly assumed a prone firing position next to the rifle. She slid a rather small scope onto the rifle and looked through it at the target.

This should be interesting, I thought. I couldn't help but to think she was showing off. Despite that, I would be impressed if she hit the target. I re-positioned my hearing protectors. Without any warning, she fired off four rounds in less than ten seconds. I couldn't tell if she hit the target or not. She set the rifle down and started to stand up. She looked awkward again, and I remembered half of one leg was missing. What looked awkward to me was simply the process she used.

"I need you to use the bike and go down and retrieve the target."

"Does it work?" I asked. It looked rusty and old.

"Of course, but it's difficult for me."

I doubted if anything would be difficult for her, but my curiosity had been aroused. I wanted to have a close look at the target. Sand and other debris fell off the bike as I picked it up off the ground. The seat felt a little loose, and the entire bike gave me the impression it might fall apart as I pedaled toward the target.

At first, it looked like only one round had struck the target. A large hole scarred the center of the plate. I removed the plate from the two by four piece of wood to which it had been stapled and studied the hole. I couldn't be sure but it looked like more than one round went through the hole. An idea came to me, and I leaned in closer to the two by four post. In the wood, I could clearly see the partial edges of four rounds bunched together to make one larger hole.

Chapter 26

Driving home, my mind bounced around among too many thoughts. If the threat to Jessie was imminent, and I believed it was, what could be done? Did Mickie really hold me responsible for keeping Jessie alive? How was I supposed to do that? And what about her? Mickie was a war hero, proven in battle, and damn lethal with any type of weapon. If she cared so much about Jessie, and I believe she did, why wouldn't she go out and stay with her?

I tried to guess how the assault on Jessie might begin. The house didn't have any nearby neighbors, so the killers could come during daylight. Move in quick, kicking the door in and killing everyone except Jessie. However, night would give them more cover. My money was on a night assault. That seemed to be their modus operandi, too.

The fact that Mickie had asked for me to come see her two days after we had just been together also had me worried. I didn't know for sure, but I didn't believe that the FBI or the state had ever placed too many resources in or around Melrose. So, what difference did it make if the few individuals they had loitering in the area were redirected north to where the truck load of illegal immigrants had been discovered.

Josh needed to be briefed, but I wasn't sure how to do it without mentioning Mickie and her source. I let that worry me for all of about ten seconds before I came up with a simple answer. I could tell Josh that I had been thinking about the situation a lot and was certain the killers would return in the next week or two. If he still needed some convincing, which I doubted, I could tell Josh I discussed my theory with Mickie, and she agreed with me.

At home, I checked on Chubbs. He seemed to be doing fine. Out back, I inspected the work on my wall. It looked sloppy but fixed. The repaired section felt and looked solid. Another section, a few yards farther down, needed to be repaired next. No rush, I thought.

The wind picked up and dark clouds approached from the west. I didn't recall the weatherman on the local channel mentioning rain, but I'd always thought by downplaying the chances of rain, the weathermen and women improved their long-term accuracy.

Inside, I checked my phone and saw that I hadn't missed any texts or calls. Normally, I wouldn't expect any, but I was getting antsy. Mickie's two-week window of high probability that the killers would return had already begun. The fact that I was willingly sticking myself in front of that window went against my normal behavior. At least, that's what I kept telling myself.

I decided to head out to Melrose early. They said late afternoon, but I thought I could kill a few hours doing something productive. Mickie had gotten me too riled up to sit still and wait. It took me thirty minutes to reach Cobb's truck stop. Despite knowing they'd snatched Cobb from the truck stop, I had not checked it out. In fact, to my recollection, while I had driven by it many times over the years, I had never been there.

Driving once again by Cannon AFB, I felt a pull for the old days when ironically life seemed a little safer. Maybe that was because I never felt alone. I resisted the temptation to drive onto the base and kill some time at the base exchange.

Like many truck stops, Cobb's had a dining area in which three national fast-food chains offered their finest to travelers. I ordered the fried chicken and fries combo.

"Grab a table, I'll bring it out to you," a middle-aged woman who looked like she'd kill for a vacation said to me. She appeared to be working alone behind the Taco Bell counter.

Of the ten or so tables in the big room, only one had a person at it. He sat near the corner with his back to the rest of the room. I selected the closest table to me and sat down. A few minutes later, the woman carried a tray with my order on it out to my table.

"Here you go," she said as she set the tray down. "Let me know if you want a refill or anything else."

"Thanks, have you got a second?"

Her smile instantly disappeared. She must have realized it, too, and forced a small smile to reappear. "Depends."

"Don't worry, I'm not selling anything, nor do I want you to do anything. I'm working with the Sheriff's office and trying figure out what happened to Mr. Cobb."

"We all know what happened. He's dead." She took a step backwards.

"Please, give me five minutes." I motioned to the chair opposite me.

She looked around. No one paid us any attention, and no one else had entered the food court. I thought she might turn around and return to the safety behind the counter, but she sat across from me.

"I don't know anything," she said.

"I understand he was abducted from the back lot. Is that what you've heard?"

"Yes, the police know that."

"I'm aware of their findings. I'm trying to work it backwards now, retracing steps. It may be a waste of time, but it's just time."

"Time I've got," she said.

"What are the theories as to why Cobb was abducted? I imagine it's been a topic of conversation here."

Once she started talking, I had no trouble keeping her talking. Unfortunately, she could provide nothing new. She did pass me on to a friend of hers who worked in the truck stop's small store. Supposedly, this friend was the go-to person for information of all types related to Melrose. She took a second away from her duties to introduce me to her friend.

Her friend, who immediately introduced herself as Taylor, was full of wild ideas and gossip. She was fun to talk to. However, other than learning the names of about twelve local women whom Cobb allegedly had sex with in his office, of all places, I learned nothing that helped. I discarded the theory that an irate husband had killed him.

I drove around to the back of the large lot and tried to envision how the abduction went down. By the time I drove away, I had to admit to myself I had been clutching at straws.

Despite being an hour or so early, I found myself driving toward Jessie's place. I pulled off the road about a mile short of her driveway. The old county road didn't have a shoulder, but the flat ground adjacent to it consisted of hard packed caliche and served just as well. I stepped out of the car and studied the terrain, trying to come up with some idea how the killers might approach the house. Nothing came to me. Despite the distance I could see the trees next to Jessie's house. I could also see six or seven antelope grouped together about a half mile off to my right.

The wind had picked up and a series of large dark clouds moved in from the west. They didn't seem organized enough to bring any rain. A gust of wind blew dust and fine sand into my face, making me turn away.

I returned to my car, did a U-turn, and went back the way I had come. In a little more than a quarter mile, I turned left on an even older and more rundown county road. Theoretically, the road should lead me to something. After traveling at a slow speed for what I imagined to be about a half of a mile, I stopped again and got out of my car. Despite my belief that the terrain was as flat as a table top, the ground here put me a little higher than Jessie's house. The antelope were now directly between the house and me.

I continued driving down the road only to discover that for two miles it continued straight before it reached a dry gulch. An old wooden barrier placed in the middle of the road blocked anyone from driving further. It didn't take much imagination to see that a flood had washed out the road some years, perhaps decades, ago.

Driving back, I noticed a trail that led away from the road in the direction of Jessie's house. I stopped the car and followed the trail on foot. Other than getting a feel for the area around Jessie's house, and maybe coming up with some theory about how the killers might sneak up on her, I didn't have a plan.

The trail came to an abrupt stop about where I had seen the antelope. A thought came to mind that the trail had been created by years of cattle treading back and forth on it. I looked around for any evidence to support my theory and discovered the scant remains of a house or possibly a small barn that had burned to the ground years earlier. The sight made me wonder if I was on private property. I looked back at Jessie's house and saw a couple small mounds that a shooter could possibly hide behind, but these guys weren't going to try to pick anyone off from a distance. They needed to get up close and personal.

A series of prairie dog mounds spread across the terrain near the remains of the burned structure. Four prairie dogs stood next to the safety of their burrows and watched me. I often thought that there were a lot more prairie dogs than people living in New Mexico.

I started walking back to my car when my phone rang.

"Jim, is that you out wondering around?" Josh asked.

I stopped and looked back toward the house. I couldn't see anyone.

"I'm inside looking out the window."

"Guilty," I said. "I'm trying to get my hands around all this."

"Why don't you come to the house. I've done a lot of that already. Our afternoon plans got changed, and I'm here by myself."

"Okay, I'll be there in a few minutes."

Feeling a little bit like I was caught snooping, I walked to the car and drove to Jessie's house.

Chapter 27

Josh stood next to a dark blue Ford Escape in Jessie's front yard and waved at me as I turned onto the driveway. I parked behind the Escape.

"Your car?" I asked as I stepped out of mine.

"Yes, have you not seen it yet?"

"No, it's nice."

He grinned, obviously proud of his small SUV. "I took a day off to help finish the installation of Jessie's security system. We were also going to the lake, but that got nixed."

I wasn't sure which lake. There was nothing nearby. I looked at the front of the house and saw a security camera above the front door.

"That's one of the cameras. Come with me, I'll show you the rest." He led me on a slow walk around the house, pointing out a wall mounted camera on each side. "They work off the wi-fi and provide pretty good coverage of the yard and beyond. They also notify you if they pick something up within twenty-five yards. I'm thinking about decreasing that to fifteen on the sides of the house to eliminate all the pinging at night. There are a lot of critters out here."

"Did they pick me up all the way out where I was?"

"No, they aren't that good. I was watching a small herd of antelope with my binoculars and happened to see you. Come on in, I'll show you what else we've done."

I followed him and noticed he was wearing the same jeans as

Friday night but had changed into a plain, black tee shirt. The jeans had a small white stain or blemish on the rear, right pocket. I wondered if he had spent the last two nights here. He stopped me at the front door.

"New lock," he said, pointing out a new heavy-duty padlock.

"Looks sturdy."

"We've got the same lock on the back door. I'm still trying to figure what to do with the windows. They all have locks, but they aren't great. I'm thinking of simply placing a steel rod at the top that could be swung down and block the window from being pushed upwards."

"Seems like that would work," I said.

"Yeah, but she's got a lot of windows and different sizes," he said as we walked into the kitchen.

"Has she been thinking any more about getting a dog?"

Josh smiled. "Yes, but she wants a puppy. Understandable, but it won't provide any protection for months. I worry she may not have that long."

"We need to talk about that."

"Okay. We can sit here at the table. Want a drink?"

"A diet soda if she has one."

Without responding he retrieved a diet Dr. Pepper for me and a Mountain Dew for himself.

"We've got you covered. Something to munch on?"

"No, thanks. The more I've been thinking about this situation, the more I keep thinking that the next week or so is the critical period."

Josh nodded but remained silent. I continued, summarizing my conversation with Mickie but without mentioning her and implying the theory was mine alone.

"You mean to tell me that the FBI has moved the two guys they've had down here to Albuquerque? I haven't heard that."

"I didn't know they had two agents here," I said.

"I don't know where they were staying, but in the past week, they'd stop by here almost every day. They were just checking up, but they said they were keeping an eye on the place."

"I'm glad to hear it," I said. "My understanding, though, is that the seizure of a large truckload of illegals, along with the arrest of two traffickers, has caused both the FBI and the state to pull their people back to Albuquerque."

"Makes sense, really. They couldn't do much here. I never saw them parked in front of the house. It may not matter."

"So, where's Jessie today?"

"The Richardson's called. One of their mares was about to give birth. Jessie left here all excited. She said I could go, too, but that's nothing I need to see." He scrunched up his face. "She said she wouldn't be late."

"That's alright. Was that a new grill out back?" I had seen it when he gave me a tour around the house.

"Yes, come look at it."

I followed him outside.

"It uses propane and has a lot of space to cook things. It even has a side burner. I guess you can put most anything in a pot and heat it up over there while you grill your meat. I'm not sure that I'll ever use it."

"My grill looked shiny and clean like this long ago, too. Now it's a mess," I said. "Still works, though."

"I can't wait to use it. Today, I thought we'd have something simple, like maybe hamburgers and hot dogs. Jessie said that would be fine with her. I hope that's okay with you, too."

"Of course it is. Can I run to the store and get anything?"

"Nothing. Jessie and I spent the morning shopping." After he said this, his expression changed and he blushed a little. "I guess you should know I spent the night here. We agreed that I should move in. I think I love her, Jim."

"Well, congratulations. I think you two make a good couple."

"I'm still trying to get my mind around it. I've been with plenty of women, of course, but I've never lived in the same place with one. Other than my sisters, of course."

I almost teased him about using the word 'plenty.' "You two will do fine. I imagine if you start to screw something up, Jessie will tell you. She seems pretty sharp to me."

Josh grinned. "She will at that." He didn't elaborate.

He started fiddling with his phone and then turned the screen around, so I could see the display. I saw the two of us standing by the grill. I was looking at his phone.

"The security camera?"

"Yes," he said. "Come back inside, and I'll show you how it can be displayed on my laptop." He started walking before I responded. Inside, he went to the kitchen and sat down at a small round table in the corner. "Come look."

I did and saw four separate pictures, each corresponding to the view from a different security camera. The pictures were quite clear. "That's impressive," I said. I was thinking of telling him the back yard camera didn't catch anyone standing close to the back door.

"What do we have here?" Josh said.

The front yard security camera gave us a view of a white utility van coming down the driveway toward the house. Without saying a word, he went outside to meet the van. I followed him. He didn't seem too concerned, but my paranoid streak came alive. I knew Josh wasn't armed. His pistol and holster were still on the kitchen counter.

The van came to a stop about twenty yards from the house. As I stepped outside, both the driver's door and the passenger door opened. I put my hand under my windbreaker and felt my Beretta in my shoulder holster. The driver stepped out of the car but stayed behind the door.

A few seconds later, the passenger got out on his side carrying something in his hand. I placed my right hand back inside my windbreaker.

"Is Jessica Perez here?"

Chapter 28

"What do you want her for?" Josh asked.

"We have a package for her," the man said. He walked steadily toward Josh but wasn't making eye contact.

"She's not here, but I can sign for it."

"Good enough for us. Are you Josh Dillard?"

"Yes."

"Then please sign this," the man said and held out a small device.

Josh did, and the man handed him the box he had tucked under his arm.

"Thanks, have a good day," the man said and went back to the van. The two men got into the van and drove it away.

Josh turned and looked at me. "That was interesting. I wonder how he knew who I was."

I shook my head. "Who is the box from?"

Josh studied the box and turned it over. "It doesn't say."

"Now, that's interesting. But it is addressed to Jessie, right?"

Josh handed me the box. It was heavier than I expected. Jessie's address was clearly displayed, but I couldn't locate any return address either.

"What do you think?" Josh asked.

"A belated birthday gift?"

"Could be."

Josh's phone chimed in his pocket. He looked at it and grinned. "It's Jessie. She said a box might be delivered today to the house, and that I could sign for it."

"Good timing."

"I'll let her know it arrived," he said and started tapping a response on his phone.

I wondered what was in the box, and who sent it. Most delivery companies require a return address.

"The guy who delivered must be with a private company," I said once Josh placed his phone back in his pocket. "I didn't see any markings on the van."

"Out here, we have people who contract with FedEx and UPS to deliver stuff for them, so some of these same people may also have their own companies. Not enough work around here for the big companies to dedicate many resources."

"Makes sense. Did Jessie indicate who the box was from?"

"Yes, Mickie."

"Then I know what it is," I said.

"What?"

"A gun, most likely a semi-automatic pistol that Mickie thinks is just right for Jessie. Knowing Mickie, I can't think of what else she would send." Actually, I could see Mickie sending survival food or a K-bar knife, but it didn't fit this scenario.

"Wish we could open it and have a look," Josh said.

"We'll get to see it soon enough. When do you expect her home? Did she say?"

"No, but earlier she said she wouldn't be late. If you don't mind, Jim, you can help me with one last project I was hoping to get done today."

"Sure," I said, hoping he didn't expect a lot of expertise.

We walked over to the back of his Ford Escape. He leaned into the trunk, and after moving some blankets aside, he retrieved a box. After dusting it off with his hand, he said, "I want to replace the old light fixture by the front door with this."

The exterior of the box had a picture of an outdoor light fixture that did look a lot nicer than the old one by the door. That one had probably been installed when the house was built, decades ago.

"That shouldn't be hard," I said.

"I'd like to get it done before Jessie gets back. She knows I'm doing it, but it will impress her more if it's up and working when she gets here."

"Let's do it," I said, feeling my enthusiasm already starting to fade. Most projects I take on end up with one or two surprises that turn a five-minute operation into a day long one. Something nagged at me that this one would be no different.

We removed the fixture, extra items and the instructions from inside the box while sitting at the kitchen table. Everything was there. We glanced through the instructions, more so to say later that we had, rather than to actually read them. After all, we were two grown men.

Outside, we ran immediately into our biggest challenge. We could not find any way to remove the fixture from the wall. We were able to gain access and remove the light bulb, but beyond that, we were stymied. A round metal plate pressed against the brick wall, covering whatever screws fastened the old fixture to the electric box.

Two, maybe three, layers of black paint made finding the small screw used to secure the plate nearly impossible. Josh spent a good five minutes scraping at the paint until he finally found it. Then it took a fair amount of WD-40 and patience before he could loosen the screw. That allowed him to pull the cover away from the wall.

Following that, he had to fight with four old and slightly rusted screws to detach the fixture itself. After considerable swearing and scraped knuckles, we were ready to separate the wires. I say we, because I was there supervising. I had also been the one who turned off the light switch. We had discussed searching for the fuse box, but decided turning the switch off would suffice.

I held the new light up close to its final position, so Josh could connect the wiring and fasten the fixture to the house. We both stood back a few steps to admire our work.

"Looks a lot better," Josh said.

"It does." The light fixture looked a little slanted, but I thought I would keep my opinion to myself.

"I'll get the light bulb," he said and went into the house.

I heard a motorcycle in the distance and looked down the road for Jessie.

"That's probably her now," Josh said. He had a light bulb in his hand that he hurriedly screwed into place. He must have turned the switch back on because the light lit up. "This can be turned off and on by the inside switch, or we can leave it turned on but move this button, and it will come on at dark and go off in the morning." The light went off. "So far, so good."

Seconds later, Jessie came into view, waving at us.

Josh walked out to the driveway to welcome her. I waited by the front door. They hugged, and Jessie started to tell him about the new colt. I could hear most of what she said. They walked toward me.

"You should have seen it, Jim. It was so beautiful!"

"I bet it was," I said, not meaning it. Watching a mare give birth wasn't something that had ever made it close to my bucket list.

"It turned out to be a filly. I don't know why they thought it would be a colt. She is so cute. Josh, you need to go with me tomorrow."

"I will," he said.

"You should come, too," she said to me.

"If I can. Look at what Josh installed for you today." I held my hand out, palm up, pointing at the new light.

"I like it."

"Jim helped."

"Very little," I said.

"It turns itself on at dark and then back off when the sun comes up."

She gave Josh a quick kiss. "Thank you."

Chapter 29

"Stop worrying," Vic said. He kept their speed right at the speed limit as they headed north.

"I know, but I just can't help thinking our driving another white van up this same stretch of highway might not be smart. We don't know if that cop got off a description of our van. Now to drive right by the spot so soon in a matching white van, you know, it's bugging me."

"You know how many white vans are out there? That's why we use them." Vic didn't give Carlos time to answer.

"I know."

"I know you're superstitious."

"Me?" Carlos said and grinned. "You're the one who's named his machete and talks to it."

Both men laughed. However, they became quiet and serious when they drove by the exact spot where they had murdered the highway patrol officer earlier in the month.

"You think she'll be alone?" Carlos asked a few seconds later.

"Probably not. A young woman that age has a boyfriend or two. I worry more about any dogs."

"We'll have to drive by once or twice to get a feel for the place. The address we have should be good."

They had discussed their plan more than once. Unless they encountered a large gathering at the house, their plan was simple. Go straight in as fast as they could and kill everyone but the girl. They brought plenty of firepower with them. If they found the girl alone, they could take their time. If no one was home, they would hide the van and search the house while waiting for the girl to return.

"If we find her alone, after we're finished, I think it might be a good idea to hide her body elsewhere," Vic said.

"Not leave her there?"

"Right. That will give us more time before she is found. If we bury her somewhere, they may never find her."

"Good idea. We could bury her in the old Meza place," Carlos said. "I often wondered how many bodies are buried out there."

Vic grinned, "One of ours, but I'm sure there are others."

The Meza place was an abandoned farm north of Roswell. Other than an old abandoned brick factory, nothing was near it. The county road that ended just past the factory had deteriorated to such an extent that no one used it anymore.

"I think we're going to get lucky tonight," Carlos said.

Either way, this trip should end their efforts to recover the necklace. They would have to lay low for a while, but neither of them minded that. Earlier that morning, Lara had informed them that the first half of the year was turning out to be the best one yet for the company. She also thought their idea to set up a branch office in Alamogordo was a great plan. She estimated the new office could increase their annual profits by fifteen percent. Vic and Carlos had so little involvement in the operations of their company, neither had any idea how much fifteen percent translated to in actual dollars, but it still sounded good.

They both received a notice from their bank at the end of each month that showed how much money had been deposited into company's management payroll account. The same notice showed how the money was split into payments to separate accounts that belonged to each of the two men and Lara.

The three had agreed on the amounts shortly after the company's start up. Forty percent for each of the men and twenty percent to Lara. None of the three had expected the monthly payouts to become as big as they had. The transparency of the process also precluded tensions that could have otherwise developed.

They stopped at a gas station at the outskirts of Melrose. After filling the gas tank, they parked the van next to the small building and went inside. As expected, the lobby had been converted into a convenience store.

"Looks like everything we need for a good dinner," Carlos said, grabbing a pack of beef jerky and two double-packed packages of peanut butter cups.

Vic went for a large beef stick and a large Baby Ruth candy bar. They agreed to share a half gallon of sweet tea. Their rule was no alcohol before a job. Tonight, that meant nothing until after the body was buried. The rule had served them well throughout the years.

Chapter 30

Carlos parked the van behind an old, self-service car wash. The car wash had four stalls, but all them were empty and appeared dry.

"I doubt if it works anymore. I'll go look to see if anyone's in the office," Vic said.

The office looked like a small wooden shed with a window. Vic walked over to it, looked through the window, and returned.

"Nobody. If we put coins in the control box by one of those stalls, the water could come on, I guess."

"Let's only try if someone shows up and gets nosy," Carlos said. "I'm eating." He opened the first of his two packages of peanut butter cups.

Vic opened the back of the van, lifted the floor mat, and opened a panel. He lifted out an old AR-15 modified to fire automatically. After ensuring it was loaded and ready to use, he wrapped it in a blanket before laying it on the floor of the van behind the front seats. Next, he removed his machete, already wrapped in a beach towel. He placed it next to the AR-15 and covered both with an old tarp stained with brown paint.

Carlos didn't have to prep. He already had his Glock 9mm semi-automatic pistol hidden under his seat. However, he doubted they would need any of the firearms. They had a fair chance of finding the girl alone, and if she had a male friend there with her, they wouldn't waste any time before killing him. Carlos knew most people who lived in these rural areas had at least one gun in their home, but more than likely the gun was stashed away somewhere and not loaded. Additionally, people were hesitant to shoot. He wasn't. If they ever did shoot first, it was usually a warning shot. The thought made him chuckle. Fools.

Vic climbed back into the driver's seat and opened his large beef stick. "Why do you eat your dessert first?"

Carlos grinned. "First and last course," he said, holding up his second, still wrapped package. "It should start getting dark in an hour or so. I suggest we stay right here until then."

"Okay with me."

Just as the sun began to disappear to the west, a black or dark blue van drove into the car wash's parking lot. It hesitated on the other side of the wash stables before slowly driving around to their side. The two men watched the van but kept their heads back against the side panels to make it hard for anyone in the other van to see much of them.

However, the two people in the dark van didn't seem to be concerned about someone seeing them. Both seemed more curious to see who might be in the white van. As the dark van drove by, both Carlos and Vic could see the reflection of a young man and woman in their side mirrors.

"I think we may have messed with their plans to have a private moment out here," Carlos said.

"Five dollars says they won't leave. If he got her to agree to come out here, he's not going to give up just because there's another van here. When you were his age, you wouldn't," Vic said.

Carlos grinned. "No, let's see."

They watched as the dark van slowed to a stop about twenty yards away. It remained there for about a minute before driving off.

"Cowards," Vic said.

"He probably knows a half dozen places he can take her. Always have a fallback plan. Remember that time at Gantry's?"

Vic smiled and nodded.

They had finished eating, and Carlos poured the last of the tea into two old plastic Allsup's cups they had brought with them in the van. "After we're done tonight, let's hit that bar you like in Portales. Maybe your girl, Issy, will be there."

Vic grinned. "My girl? I think you like her more than I do."

They talked about women and their favorite bars. Nobody else drove into the car wash lot. As the last of the sunlight finally faded away, Vic started the engine.

"Let's do this," he said.

They drove east through the small town. Neither of them glanced at Cobb's Truckstop, although Carlos wondered if it might have a new name soon. He felt no remorse or other emotions over their killing of Cobb. He tried to think back and remember if he had ever felt any remorse over any of his killings. He couldn't remember a time when he had. Of course, he could no longer remember all the times he had killed someone. That was probably normal, he thought.

He could remember how many times Jack, their go-between with the large crime families in the country, had tasked them with killing someone. Only eight times, no nine times, he recalled. How could he forget the trip to Juarez?

"What are you thinking of?" Vic asked.

"The job in Juarez. The one Jack sent us to do."

"That was my favorite."

Vic had said that before. Carlos could never tell if he was

serious or joking. In Juarez, death had them both in its grip, and how they survived was still a mystery to him. Bad shooting was all he could think of.

"We were lucky to live through that one."

"We're invincible," Vic said.

Carlos knew better. Jack had sent them to Juarez to find and kill Leon Dominguez. Leon had ripped off someone he shouldn't have. Jack rarely explained things unless they were tasked to recover something. In Juarez, the mission simply called for Leon's death. Jack gave them sufficient information to locate Leon and a recent photograph.

Operating in Mexico brought with it a number of extra problems. Fortunately, language was not one of them as both men could speak fluent Spanish. They were able to find Leon and come up with a plan. Unfortunately, the plan wasn't a very good one, and they both knew it. Leon seemed to know that someone would be coming for him. He lived upstairs over a popular restaurant that had a large bar counter. Everyone who worked there knew him. In the three days they watched the building, Leon never left.

On a few occasions while inside the restaurant, they watched as Leon went through a door marked "private" and did not return. A young waitress, who became chatty with Vic, told them that the door led to stairs that went upstairs to offices and apartments where the family who owned the place lived. No one but the family and a few others were allowed to go up there.

While they could get close to Leon in the restaurant, there were too many witnesses. Plus, two tough looking guys hung around inside. One stood by the front door and the other by the door to the upstairs. They remained there for most of the day. A local policeman maintained a presence out front.

Vic and Carlos had brought pistols into Mexico but had kept them well concealed in their old Toyota. This was no place for a U.S. citizen to be caught with firearms.

The two men spent each day at the restaurant for lunch, and then after six, when they sat at the bar for a couple hours. In between and for a few hours afterwards, they watched the entrance to the restaurant from various nearby spots. The finally decided they had to make their move while they were inside. The best time to do it would be when Leon left the restaurant to go upstairs. They would intercept him while he went through the doorway and kill him just beyond the door. The guard would likely try to stop them, but they planned to pull or push the guard past the door and kill him, too. That way no one in the restaurant would see anything.

Of course, there were two variables they had no control over. First, they didn't know what was beyond the door. While they could see what looked like a hallway when the door was opened, they could only see a few yards past the door. Second, they knew the guard had a handgun tucked under his shirt, and they thought Leon would at least be armed with a knife.

Still, they had a job to do, and they both agreed a hundred grand for finishing the job was too much to walk away from. Carlos and Vic entered the restaurant at seven in the evening. Instead of sitting at the bar counter, the two men sat at the table adjacent to the door. If Leon kept up his routine, around eight, he would get up from his table and leave through this door.

They ordered a light dinner and waited. As expected, after about an hour, Leon stood and started walking toward them. For whatever reason, the tough guy guarding the door opened it for

Leon this time, and the two started talking.

Vic and Carlos rose as Leon reached the door. Leon laughed at something the guard said. Neither noticed until the last minute that Vic and Carlos had approached them. Catching the two off-guard, Vic grabbed Leon and pushed him through the door. Carlos did the same with the guard a second later. In one fluid motion, Carlos closed the door behind him with his right hand, pulled his knife out, and jammed it into the guard's solar plexus. He repeated the stab twice more before he let go of the guard's shirt and watched him slide to the floor. Only then did he see the pistol in the guard's right hand.

He turned his attention to Vic and saw him gently place Leon on the floor. Blood gushed from similar stab wounds on Leon. An image appeared at the top of the stairs and a man shouted. Carlos couldn't remember what the man said, because when he looked up all he could see was a huge hole staring back at him. The hole was at the deadly end of a large revolver that suddenly roared into action.

The two men instinctively crouched. Trapped, they both heard three or four rounds streak by them and rip holes into the door. Carlos's hand was on the guard's pistol before he realized he had reached for it. He fired one round at the man at the top of the stairs. The man fell and rolled down the stairs toward them.

They heard shouting behind them and imagined the policeman and the other guard were out there waiting to see what happened. They heard people talking in frightened voices above them, too. Any moment more armed individuals would show up to see what had happened. They had to move.

"The window," Carlos said. He pointed to the window at the top of the stairs.

The two dashed upstairs. A second set of stairs reversed back and led up to the second floor. They found the window locked but only with the manufacturer's clasps. Vic snapped them open and raised the window, discovering no screen and an alley that sat eight feet below them. Someone shouted from above them, calling out a name. Vic and Carlos didn't hang around. The two climbed out the window and dropped, landing uninjured on the alley. They sprinted to the narrow road that passed behind the restaurant.

They ran until they reached another main road. This put them a couple hundred yards away from the restaurant and on a busy street with plenty of other pedestrians. From there they walked two more blocks to where they had parked their car. They crossed the border into the United States ten minutes later.

Chapter 31

Inside, Josh showed Jessie the box that had come for her. She picked it up and smiled. "Can you guess what it is?" Josh asked.

"I think so. Mickie sent it to me," she grinned.

"Open it," Josh said.

"Not yet. I really, really need a shower. I'll be quick," she said and left the room.

"I wish she would've opened the box. I'm interested to see what it is," Josh said.

"You don't think it's a pistol?"

"It probably is, but what type?"

"Good point," I said.

"I wish Mickie would've come out here for the barbeque tonight or to Jessie's birthday party. I know she likes her privacy, but I'd like to meet her."

"She's just another person, Josh. Besides, she says she never leaves her property anymore. I imagine she does but not very often."

"I know. I asked Jessie to invite her out today, but she said Mickie wouldn't come, and the invite would annoy her. I guess she's one of those hermits."

I smiled. "That she is."

"Let's go start the grill. We won't put the hamburgers on until Jessie gives us the thumbs up. We have hot dogs, too."

He had already told me that, but I figured he was a little

nervous. I didn't know if he had much grilling experience and could be concerned that I might be critical. Of course, he could have been more concerned about what Jessie might think of his grilling skills.

For my part, I was already feeling like the proverbial third wheel. I had to keep telling myself I was there to help protect Jessie. I knew at some point I would have to leave. They wouldn't want me there all night, nor did I come prepared to stay. I planned to stay until it became obvious to all of us that I needed to leave. Then, I would keep my fingers crossed nothing happened after I left.

The sun had started its daily disappearing act in the west, and the air had become cooler. The grill heated up quickly. We both edged closer to it.

"There's your antelope again," I said, pointing to a small herd of them in the distance. "I doubt if there's much meat on them."

Josh laughed. "Can't hunt them anyway. The warmth from the grill feels good, don't you think?"

Jessie walked out, wearing blue jeans and a white, pullover blouse that didn't quite reach the jeans. I knew it was the current style, but at night, outside, I thought it would be just as attractive to mosquitoes as it was to the opposite sex. Then again, I knew styles rarely concerned themselves with practicality.

The two hugged again, and I found myself watching the headlights of a vehicle on the road that ran in front of Jessie's house. I walked off to the side to see if it would drive by. It did. Still, the hairs on the back of my neck demanded attention. I rubbed them to calm them and myself down.

"You don't have to sneak away, Jim. We were just hugging. We won't do it again," Jessie said. She looked happy and still hung on to Josh's hand.

"I saw a white van drive by, like the one that delivered the item earlier. I was just watching to see if you got another delivery."

"I doubt it," she said.

"How about I toss on the hamburgers, and you get your box and open it," Josh said.

"Curious, aren't you?" Jessie teased.

"Yes, of course, and hungry."

"Okay then," she said and went back inside. Josh followed her but came out first. He had all six hamburgers on the grill before she reappeared.

"I took it out of the wrapping paper. Look how nice this box is." Jessie held out a dark, shiny wooden box.

I didn't see any markings on it. To me it looked like a larger than normal, fancy cigar box. I don't smoke, but I had seen similar boxes that my friends in the past would break out late at night to offer guests a cigar. I had made the mistake of accepting a cigar or two, along with a few glasses of cognac at one or two in the morning. The results for me were never very pleasant.

She positioned herself underneath the light on the back wall of the house and opened the box. We moved in close enough to see inside the box once she opened it.

"It's heavy. Would you hold it, Josh, while I take it out?"

The "it" she referred to was a pistol, a little smaller than my Beretta but still lethal. Jessie removed it, keeping the barrel aimed at the ground.

"It's not loaded, is it?" Josh asked.

I felt certain Mickie wouldn't have sent a loaded weapon to Jessie, but I kept quiet. I didn't like thinking that Jessie needed one, either. The world has never been as safe as we would like to believe. For Jessie, the evil in the world had indeed become personal.

She handed the pistol to Josh and took the box from him. He checked to make sure the weapon was empty and balanced it in his hand.

"It's sweet," he said.

"Put it back in the box, please. We don't need it out tonight," she said. "Oh, wait, there's a note." She took a small envelope out of the box before setting the box down on the table next to the grill. She opened the envelope and read it.

"What does it say?" Josh asked.

"Here," Jessie said and handed him the letter. She smiled at me.

"Happy birthday, call me, and we can set up a time for me to teach you how to use this. She just signed it with an M."

Josh looked inside the box. "No bullets."

"I think she wants to teach me how to use it before she gives me any bullets."

"That makes sense," I said. "Your grill is starting to flame up on the hamburgers."

Josh turned around and immediately grabbed a plastic, spray bottle. He handed me the pistol.

"It's not bad," he said. He set the spray bottle back down and flipped the hamburgers. This action caused the grill to flame up again, so he sprayed a little water over the spot where the flames were most active.

"You may want to put this away," I said to Jessie and handed her the pistol.

She took it without comment and placed it back into its box.

"I'll be right back, Josh. Don't burn our hamburgers."

I thought I heard her giggling as she went inside. In the distance, I saw a pair of headlights appear and then disappear. Despite several plausible explanations for such an occurrence, it bothered me. I knew I was getting jumpy, and I didn't like the feeling.

"Those hamburgers look delicious, Josh," I said. They did, but my comments were as much to get my mind off the threat as to complement him.

"I hope they are. Will you eat two?"

"Is the sky blue?"

He grinned. "I'm making two for myself, too."

"Do we want to eat outside?" Jessie asked from just inside the door.

"I suggest we eat inside," I said before Josh had a chance to respond.

"Inside is fine," Josh said.

When Jessie disappeared inside, I said, "I kind of feel like a sitting duck out here in the dark under this light."

"Good thought," he said.

"I know I'm overreacting, but it's good practice."

Chapter 32

"I saw a couple people in the backyard. Looked like they were barbequing something. Before we leave the house, we may want to grab some dinner to go," Carlos said and laughed to himself.

"Yeah, I saw that, too. I think I saw two men, so that would make three of them if the girl is there," Vic said.

"The more the merrier. I hope they were barbequing chicken. That's my favorite."

"Not ribs? Hell, I'd even take a hamburger over chicken."

"So, if it's chicken, we don't take some for you?"

"I didn't say that," Vic said and laughed.

"How much longer should we wait?"

"Not much."

"Yeah, I agree. If someone drives by, we may look suspicious. I say we go in ten minutes. Fifteen max," Carlos said.

"We park in the driveway and go at the door fast. If someone other than the girl comes out to meet us, we'll put him down. Quiet, if possible, but we need to be prepared to shoot and move. We take the girl alive. If we haven't made too much noise, we can take our time in the house with her. If we have to shoot our way in, we grab her and take her somewhere in the van. We need to be certain that she tells us where the necklace is if she knows."

"Or we need to be certain she knows nothing. Afterwards, we can leave her out in the desert somewhere under a foot of dirt and sand."

"That's the plan. You know, I'd hate to think we did all this for nothing," Vic said.

"I think if we head back that way a little, we'll be able to see if they are still out back. If someone remains by the grill we may have to split up."

Carlos nodded. "Let's hope this doesn't get too complicated."

They moved the van about a half mile closer, to a point where they could see the house in the distance. Leaving the engine running, they turned off the headlights.

"Yeah, there's three of them," Vic said after a minute. "It looks like they're looking at something. I can't tell what it is from here."

"Me neither, but one just went inside, and it looks like they're getting ready to take the food off the grill. Let's see if they all go inside before we move."

"We should've brought some binoculars."

The two sat quietly for a couple of minutes.

"You didn't see any sign of a dog, did you?" Carlos asked.

"No. You?"

"No. Looks like they're going inside. Let's get going."

Vic turned the lights back on but kept the van's speed down, making their approach as quiet as possible. Carlos studied the area around them as they drove toward the house. He saw the lights from a few scattered houses in the distance. A mile or more separated the nearest one from their target.

They turned onto the driveway and as quietly as they could let the van coast into a position behind the two cars.

"A Mustang," Vic said.

"Nice. I wanted one when I was younger, a black one with the large engine. I'm not sure why I never bought one. It was cheaper than the pickups I always ended up with."

"You loved those pickups."

"Yes, I did, but I think I would've loved a Mustang, too."

"A chick magnet. That's what you wanted. You needed one with that mug of yours. Good thing you had me around to bring them to us."

Carlos grinned but didn't respond. "Come on, let's get this over with," he said.

"Yeah, let's get to work."

Chapter 33

Once darkness arrived, Mickie selected a spot nearly four hundred yards from the house. She positioned the brown camouflage netting over herself. She anticipated a frontal assault. Her location gave her a good line of sight to both the front and back yards. She scanned the area with her binoculars and smiled when she observed Jessie's reaction to her gift.

Mickie only had to wait fifteen minutes. The van's headlights got her attention, and when it turned onto Jessie's driveway, she knew it was game-on. She had no doubt these were the killers and had to resist the urge to kill them as they got out of the van.

"Different rules here, girl," she whispered to herself. "They get to shoot first."

Chapter 34

"This reminds me of the hamburger place you took me to, Jessie. A little different, but similar," I said after taking my first bite.

"What? Freshly grilled burgers with a basket of potato chips. We had fries there, but I can see what you mean," she said. "I even have the same red-checkered, plastic table cloth."

"But the hamburgers here are much tastier," I said.

"Thanks," Josh said. "What, what's up?"

My seat at the kitchen table positioned me where I could watch the screen of the nearby laptop. The feed from the front yard security camera could be seen on it. As Josh started speaking, I watched the headlights of what appeared to be a van drive down the driveway toward us.

"Are you expecting another delivery, Jessie?" I asked.

Both Josh and Jessie turned their attention to the laptop's screen.

"No," Jessie said.

"Who could that be?" Josh said.

"I don't know," Jessie said.

"Stay here. I'll go check," Josh said.

"Be careful," Jessie said. I could sense the fear in her voice.

"I will," Josh said and picked his hip holster. He put it on and adjusted his service weapon, a Smith & Wesson 9mm semi-automatic pistol, to ensure easy access.

I stood up.

"Stay with Jess," he instructed and started for the front door.

I compromised by staying inside but by the front window to keep an eye on Josh. Two men appeared to be in the front of the van. I watched them as they got out of the van. I couldn't see any markings on the van. The driver had turned the van slightly before they stopped, so the headlights shown toward the front of the house. If they had turned the van a little more, the headlights would've made seeing the two men very difficult. I believed that was their intent, but they just didn't achieve it.

One of the men took a couple of steps toward Josh. The other lingered by the open passenger door.

"What can I do for you?" Josh called out to the men.

Neither replied, and without thinking I pulled my Beretta out of its holster. One part of my mind kept asking if I was going to shoot a delivery man. The larger part of my mind ignored the question.

"Stop right there. I'm a deputy with the sheriff's office. Stop and state your business," Josh said loud enough for me to hear. I knew the men had to have heard him. Josh started to raise his pistol, and all hell broke out.

The man closest to him drew a handgun and fired. Josh fired back, and the sound of three more shots being fired exploded in the front yard. I raced outside and saw Josh on the ground crawling toward the front door. I could tell he was seriously wounded.

The man shooting at Josh was on one knee but still shooting. He fired a round that took out the new light next to the front door, missing me by inches. I fired back while moving, but grabbed Josh to get him to safety rather than look to see if I hit anything.

Josh collapsed against me as I tried to lift him. I staggered, thinking we had both run out of time. Suddenly, another set of hands grabbed him. Jessie yanked him and pulled him toward the front door. Her help allowed me to get most of his weight balanced against me. Between the two of us we moved quickly toward the door.

Just when we reached the door, the sound of automatic gunfire erupted behind us. Chunks of the house tore away and glass shattered. I felt a sting below my right knee, and we all collapsed inside the doorway. I slammed the door shut with my foot.

"I didn't have any bullets," Jessie said. Her voice sounded choked and terrified.

"That's okay. Drag him behind the couch and try to stop the bleeding. I'll try to keep them away from us."

I knew that was not going to be easy. I went to the window. Half of the glass had already been shot out. I peeked out and saw one of the men helping the other stand up. The wounded man leaned against the van, but even in the darkness, I saw him nod to the other. Damn, I thought, two attackers, even with one injured, were a lot harder to defend against than just one.

I had to expose more of myself to get a good shot, and the light behind me must have highlighted me. Before I could get a round off, the second man opened up with his automatic rifle. I couldn't tell what it was. Maybe an AK-47, I thought, but it didn't matter. What was left of the window shattered, and I had to dive to the floor. Shards of glass and wood chips from the window frame bounced around me,

"Call 911!"

"I don't have my phone." Jessie's voice sounded muffled. I thought something may have happened to her until I realized my ears were ringing with all the gunfire.

"Here, use mine," I unlocked my cell phone and tossed it to her. It landed on the couch, and she reached over and grabbed it.

I glanced out the window again and saw the two men starting to separate. I fired at the one with the automatic weapon. He responded instantly by spraying the house with more rounds. More shattered glass, wood fragments, and even chips of bricks flew into the room. As soon as the firing stopped, I fired another shot at each of them. I ducked back down.

I could hear Jessie yelling into the phone. Her house was miles from town, and the town wasn't very big. Hopefully, one of the agencies still had some type of presence close to us. I glanced out the window and saw nothing. At least, I didn't think I saw anything. Something in the back of my mind said look again. I did and saw the men lying on the ground. Dark, uneven clumps on a dark ground. Neither moved.

"They're sending an ambulance," Jessie said.

"The police, too, I hope."

"Yes. What's happening?"

"I think I shot them," I said.

"Are you sure?"

I went to the front door and opened it. Chunks of wood from the door frame fell to the floor. Looking out, I could definitely see two bodies on the ground. I aimed and carefully squeezed off one more round into each man. Someone in the future might question the ethics of my shooting them after they were down, but that didn't matter to me at the time.

"I'm sure now."

Neither of the men reacted to my shots, so I was certain they were incapable of hurting us. Still, I walked out, keeping my eyes on them for any signs of movement. I saw none. I approached the closest one, the man with the automatic rifle.

I froze. Something wasn't right. Despite the darkness, I could see that a chunk of his face, to include his left eye, was missing. My pistol should not have done that. The face on the other man looked undamaged, but he, too, was dead. I kept my pistol in my hand and checked out the van. No one was inside. I'd leave a more thorough search for the police.

I looked around. It was now too dark to see much. Only the light coming through the windows and open front door of the house and the headlights of the van illuminated the front yard. As I started back to the house, something on the edge of the driveway caught my eye. I picked it up and put it in my pocket. I looked again into the darkness. It might have been my imagination, but in the distance, I thought I saw a shadow in the dark.

Sirens from the first responders' vehicles broke the silence. I placed my Berretta back in its holster and hoped they were in time to save Josh.

Chapter 35

Mickie walked faster than was safe in the darkness on the hard, uneven, dirt trail. As she did, she took the rifle apart and placed it in the large duffel bag that already contained the two used shell casings. The bag muffled the noise of the pieces clanging together. Still, she cursed silently to herself. Sound carried a long way out here.

She felt good. Mission accomplished early on the first night. Now she had to evade detection as she returned to her home base. Two hundred yards from where she fired the shots, she reached her bicycle. She had spent half of the morning replacing the wheels and tires and greasing anything that made a hint of a rattle. The new tires were made of solid rubber and had no tread.

She took her small night vision goggles out of a pouch attached to the bike. She put them on and rode the bike across the old county road and cross country for a mile. She encountered another county road and rode the bike north on that road to her pickup truck.

As she drove away, she noticed the flashing lights of more first responders in the distance. They were heading to Jessie's house and away from her. She had seen Josh go down and hoped he was still alive.

She needed to get away without being noticed. She had not done anything illegal, at least nothing major. The two killers had already started shooting. However, Mickie could not stomach the thought of the police going through her house and possibly taking her in for questioning.

She worried more about the press. The press would have a field day. Everyone would discover who she was and where she lived. With her imagination running wild, she envisioned a tour bus stopping at the end of her driveway, and people getting out and taking pictures.

The mission had turned out to be quite easy, she thought, forcing her mind away from visions of television cameras in her front yard. The terrain, while appearing flat, was full of gentle undulations and the occasional mound. One such mound gave her a perfect vantage point.

When it happened, it happened fast. Too fast, she thought. Only fifteen seconds separated the first shot from one of the men who came to kill Jessie, and her last shot, killing that same man. She waited and watched for another twenty seconds to ensure the two killers were down for good. She saw Jim step outside and put another round into each of them.

"Smart move," she had whispered to herself before she rose and began her retreat.

A small animal ran across the road in front of her, bringing her focus back to the present and her driving. She knew she still had work to do when she reached her home. The first thing would be to put a different barrel in the rifle. She would then switch the wheels and tires out on the bicycle replacing them with the old ones. All her clothes would go into the laundry, and she would take a long, hot shower.

The odds of the authorities coming to interview her were slim, but she needed to be ready. She would ensure that nothing the police could easily find would support a theory that she had been anywhere near Melrose tonight. She had left her phone in her kitchen, and this old pickup didn't have GPS capability. Her newer one, parked in her driveway, did.

Mickie reached her house without incident. She parked her old pickup in the large metal barn where she kept a lot of her equipment. She let half of the air out of the passenger-side, rear tire. No one would think it had been driven in a while.

She sat at a work desk and started cleaning the parts to her rifle. While she had a lot of equipment in her house, out here is where she kept her heavy-duty equipment. She replaced the rifle barrel. If the police searched her place and seized the rifle, they would not be able to connect the weapon with either of the rounds that killed the two men. A few last things to do, she thought, humming softly to herself.

Chapter 36

Inside, I found Jessie pressing a bloody towel down on Josh's chest. She was crying, and Josh was talking incoherently to her. Her white blouse had splotches of Josh's blood on it as did her hands. Blood had also stained the lower right leg of Josh's jeans around what I imagined was a bullet hole. I ran into the bathroom and came out with a towel. I tied the towel as tight as I could around the hole in his jeans. Neither Jessie nor Josh appeared to pay any attention to what I was doing.

"I hear the sirens," Jessie said. "Do you hear them, Josh. You're going to be okay. Josh, the doctor is coming."

Despite his babbling, Josh looked at her and nodded. He may have even smiled. Jessie continued to cry.

I went back into the kitchen and located a flashlight I had seen earlier. Returning outside, I figured I had about a minute to find what I was looking for.

The minute turned into two before a large fire engine pulled into the driveway. A smaller ambulance pulled in behind it. I met them as they stopped about five yards behind our attackers' van. Another set of flashing lights could be seen in the distance. The police, I thought, and wondered why the medical response entered the scene first.

"What have we got here?" asked the first person who approached me. I could see her look at the two men on the ground. She held a flashlight and used it to do a quick survey of the immediate area.

I could sense the tension in her voice.

"These two are dead. It's safe now. There's a severely wounded man inside that needs your help."

"What the hell?" A young man shouted nervously and ran up. He wore a blue wind breaker with a Curry County EMT patch on it. He carried a medium sized case in his left hand.

"Inside, hurry," the woman said to him, and he hustled off into the house.

Three more responders approached us. They seemed more interested in the appearance of the house and the bodies on the ground than getting to anyone injured.

"Harry, go inside and help Brian. You two, make sure those guys are dead. If they are, leave everything alone, the sheriff won't want us messing up his scene." The woman spoke with authority. Unlike the others, she was dressed in civilian attire.

"What happened here?" she asked.

"These two tried to kill us. They came here for Jessica Perez. She's the daughter ---"

"I know who she is," she said, cutting me off. She looked around, cussing softly to herself.

"I'm Jim West, a friend. Who are you?"

She looked back at me. "Oh yeah, sorry about that. Don't mean to be rude. It's just I haven't been to a scene like this before, and I've been working here for eleven years. I'm Xena Pearsall. My mom was young, dumb, and fascinated with that warrior princess on TV. But I've come to like my name."

I imagined the last bit of information came out of her mouth in reaction to the stressful scene and not with any forethought.

One of the men who were checking on the bodies walked up to us. "What the hell did you shoot these guys with?"

"Are they dead?" Xena asked before I had a chance to respond.

"Way dead," the second man who was told to check on the bodies said. He was still next to one of the dead men on the ground. "This guy has a big hole in his chest."

"Not our job to sort this out. We let the county do that. Go inside and see if you can be of any help. Make sure the girl's okay, too."

The two men hurried inside.

"How are you doing?" she asked me. Her voice sounded like her nerves had settled down.

"I'm okay. My ears are still ringing, and I imagine my blood pressure is a little high. I'm more concerned about Josh, the young man inside."

"Come over here and lean against the fire engine." She started to walk away. When I didn't move, she said, "I need to look at your wound."

"My wound?"

She lit up my jeans with her flashlight. Just below my knee on the side of my leg, I could see a tear. I could also see a large stain. "Blood," I said without thinking.

"Be my guess, too, Jim. Come along. Your adrenalin is messing with you. After I see what's going on, I'll need you to go inside and sit down. Don't need you fainting and busting your head open, messing up the sheriff's crime scene."

I leaned against the front of the vehicle. "Now that I know it's there, it does kind of hurt. Not much, but I'm surprised I didn't notice it before."

"Two choices: drop your jeans or let me cut them open a little. I'd prefer the cutting choice. I don't want to give these guys the wrong idea when they see me on my knees in front of you with your jeans around your ankles."

"Cut the jeans." I grinned. This woman with her short brown hair impressed me. I waved at the sheriff's vehicle as it pulled up next to the EMS wagon.

"Turn to the side," she said and pushed me.

Two deputies with weapons drawn approached us. Both took in the scene, and neither appeared relaxed.

"Everything is secure now," I said. "We have these two down for the count. They're the gunmen that came after Jessie. Deputy Josh Dillard is inside. He's been shot and is not doing well. He's the hero of the night. I believe that's his service weapon on the ground over there by the door."

"Any more of them?" the older of the two asked.

"Not that I'm aware of. You may want someone to walk around the back of the house, but these two came out of that van. No one else came with them."

"Those two dead?" he directed the question to Xena.

"Stone cold."

"You've got your team in with Deputy Dillard?"

"Of course, they should be bringing him out in a second. Brian is with him. He's the most talented of any of us. I believe the girl is uninjured. However, she's probably terrified. You guys will be here all night. Look at that mess," she aimed her flashlight at the front of the house.

"Damn," the younger of the two said.

"Did you do any of the shooting?" the older one asked.

"Yes, but not at the house. You'll probably want my pistol."

"Where is it?"

I opened my wind breaker a little wider to expose my

shoulder holster. He asked me to remove my pistol with two fingers and hand it to him. I did, and he handed it off to his partner. "Go secure this."

"Here come the rest of them," Xena said and stood up.

I saw four sets of flashing lights in the distance. A second later, the faint sound of sirens reached us.

"Jim, I only cut your jeans wide enough to see the wound. You'll need stitches, and the wound needs to be cleaned. It's just a little more than a graze, but still, you should ride along with the deputy to the hospital."

"Xena, I don't think we'll be able to separate Jessie from Josh tonight, and she'll need some observation and counseling. Besides, she didn't really see what all happened. I need to stay here and walk the police through everything."

"You may be right. Those two are that close?"

I nodded.

"I'll stay, too, and clean and wrap your leg. You can have the stitches put in tomorrow at the hospital."

"Yeah, you both should stick around," the older deputy said.

Xena's cellphone rang, making a sound like an old-fashioned home phone. She answered and said "yes" a couple of times before hanging up. "We have a helicopter enroute to take the deputy to the hospital. Should be here in about five minutes. They wanted me to reassure them it was necessary."

I assumed one of the responders inside made the call. That meant Josh was still alive. One of the EMT's stuck his head outside and called for Xena. She went inside. I waited outside for the reinforcements.

Someone must have informed the occupants of the approaching vehicles the scene was secure or that the sirens were upsetting the farm animals, because all the sirens went silent at once. They were still a minute or two out. Their flashers continued their bright display against the dark horizon.

Chapter 37

Four county vehicles brought out eleven deputies. My friend, Deputy Johnny Willis, was among them. The older deputy who had gotten to the scene earlier went up to him while the rest of the deputies spread out, waiting for instructions.

The two talked for about a minute. I could see the deputy pointing out the bodies in the front yard, the white van, pointing to me, and to the damage at the front of the house.

Johnny barked some orders to his deputies before he approached me. "Jim, how are you? I'm glad you're not lying on the ground with those two."

"Nearly was. You have a badly wounded deputy inside."

"I know. I'm heading in there right now. I'll just be in the way, but I need to go in." He looked to the east. "That should be the helicopter there."

I looked and saw it in the distance.

"Sean, come here," Johnny called out to a tall, thin deputy standing close by. "Take a preliminary statement from Jim, but first, instruct the guys to secure the scene."

"The scene?"

"Do a circle around the house. At least thirty yards out. Then set up some lights. Have them be careful. We don't want them to damage the scene, but we also don't want anyone snakebit either. Okay?"

"Yes, sir."

"Jim, I need to get inside." He turned and left. I could see he didn't want to face Josh. No doubt he blamed himself for having Josh come out here in the first place.

Once he left, Sean came up and introduced himself. "Where would you like to talk?"

"Can we hold off until after the helicopter leaves? You may want to have your guys start securing the scene, too."

The helicopter started its descent. The noise blocked out whatever Sean said to me. A rolling stretcher attended by two of the emergency response team appeared in the doorway of the house. They waited until the helicopter had landed some seventy-five yards away, before they moved toward it. Josh had an oxygen mask on and didn't appear to be moving. Jessie, with Xena's arms around her, hurried alongside. A deputy followed the group. Johnny came out and stood on the front porch watching the group depart. He looked over at me and shook his head.

My stomach knotted up. The thought of Josh dying hit me like the proverbial kick in the groin. I knew I needed to sit down.

I went inside, and Johnny followed. "They told me it didn't look good," he said, as I passed him and made my way to the couch.

"He's still breathing," I said. "He's young and tough. And, he has a reason to live."

"Jessie?"

"Yes. They're in love, and hopefully, he believes she still needs him."

Sean came inside. "Ready, Jim?"

"Can we do it here?"

"Of course," Johnny answered for him. "Now tell us what all happened tonight."

I went through everything. They only interrupted me a couple of times to clarify who was where and the timing of things. While we were talking another van arrived. A few minutes later, large construction lights illuminated the outside. The sharp edges of what was left of the glass in the front window glowed in colors like a prism.

"We need to collect all the weapons that were used tonight. We have yours. Do you know where Josh's is?"

"I told one of the deputies it was on the ground close to the front of the house. Josh had taken a few steps towards the two men when all the shooting started. I saw it when Jessie and I were carrying him inside."

"That's all? Just the two? Jessie didn't do any of the shooting?"

"No. After we got back inside, she stayed behind the couch trying to keep Josh alive." I wondered if he had been told about the larger wounds and knew there had to be more to the story.

Xena entered the house, carrying a black shoulder bag. She looked at me and the two deputies. "They're gone. He's got about a twenty five percent chance of making it, but my money is on him."

"I pray he does," Johnny said.

I nodded.

"If you're done here, I'd like to tend to my patient before he bleeds out."

Johnny looked at me and down at my bloody jeans. "That bad?"

"No, barely a flesh wound. She just wants to see my legs." My comment lightened the mood, but just barely.

A deputy entered the house and stepped around Xena. He motioned with his hand at Johnny. They both went outside, and

Sean followed a few seconds later. Xena cut the leg of my jeans at my knee and pulled it off.

"Let's go into the kitchen. It will be easier to do this there," she said.

In the kitchen, she set her bag on the table. I moved the plates over to the counter by the sink and seeing the wood box that Jessie's pistol came in, I covered it with the three place mats that were on the table. Other deputies drifted in and out and talked briefly with Xena, asking about Josh.

"This is going to mess up the floor, but considering the damage already done, this is nothing. Sit down and put your foot up in this chair," she said. She had pulled one of the chairs around, so I could sit in one and stretch my leg straight out, resting my foot in the other. She pulled another one around where she could treat my injury.

Xena spent the next ten minutes flushing and cleaning my wound and the area around it. I had a chance to get my first good look at it and didn't think it looked too bad. However, by the time she finished cleaning and treating it, the pain had become real.

"Stop squirming, I'm done. I just need to wrap it now." Before she could start, her phone rang again. Like before, she answered with a couple yesses and this time threw in a no.

Two deputies came in through the back door and looked at us for a moment before proceeding through the kitchen.

"All these interruptions do take the romance out of things," she said, shaking her head.

I knew she was joking, and I liked her sense of humor. She also had an obvious wedding ring on her left hand.

"Too tight?" she asked when she had finished wrapping my leg.

"No. You're good at this."

"I was a school nurse for twenty years, before I took this job. Now that was a tough time. You want something for the pain?"

"No, don't think so."

"Here, at least take this." Rather than hand me something, Xena went to the sink, found a clean glass, filled it with water, and brought it to me. When she handed me the glass, she also offered me a small package that contained two Tylenol. "Take it." She then stared at me until I opened the package and took my medicine. I imagined she used the same look on hundreds of school kids before me.

Deputy Johnny Willis walked into the kitchen and sat down next to me. He looked serious. Xena excused herself.

"We've got a small problem, Jim. It's more of a puzzle. I mean I can't see where anyone has done anything wrong. Yet, those two out there were definitely hit with a high-powered round that was certainly larger than the 9mm both you and Josh had with you. How could that be?"

"I have no idea. The two of us and Jessie were the only ones here, and none of us used any weapon that we have not turned over to your people."

"You know we're going to search this house."

"Please do, and while you're at it, check out my car."

He nodded at me like he heard me but couldn't quite believe me. He left, and I returned to the couch in the living room. It was going to be a long night.

Chapter 38

The Curry County sheriff and two FBI agents arrived about a half hour later. The bodies were still on the ground in front of the house, and we had not received any update on Josh. They walked the scene and were briefed by Johnny.

When they came into the house, they looked at me with curiosity. Johnny explained who I was, but no one spoke to me. Their discussion among themselves focused on how many bullet holes they could count on the interior walls.

Shortly after they went back outside, Jessie called me. I expected crying but there wasn't any.

"Jim. I heard you were shot. Are you okay?"

"Yes, my leg got grazed. They just bandaged it. How are you and Josh?"

"I'm fine. They wanted to give me something to calm me down, but I wouldn't let them. Are they still there?"

"They'll be here all night and probably longer. You may have to spend the night at your aunt's."

"I plan to. They think Josh has a good chance to make it."

"That's great."

"He's lost a lot of blood and has been hurt real, real bad, but they've got their best doctors working on him. Jim, they keep asking me who else was there with us. They didn't seem to believe me when I said it was just the three of us. I don't understand."

"Don't worry. Stick to the truth. Don't add any theories. They are saying a high-powered weapon killed the two, not the guns Josh and I were using."

"That doesn't make sense," Jessie said.

"I know. Unless some guardian angel sat out in the dark alone, in the distance, watching over you. But that would be a far-fetched theory. Bringing it up or speculating on it wouldn't do anyone any good. I didn't see anyone. Did you?"

"No." Her voice was soft like her mind was working on a theory.

"So, stick to the facts. That would be my advice. Can't go wrong with telling them what we know and leaving speculation alone."

"Do you think those two men were the ones that killed my mom?"

"Yes, I do."

"Then I'm glad they're dead."

"Me, too. I'll stay here as long as I can tonight to keep an eye on your house. I don't think the police will keep it sealed off for more than a day, maybe two."

"Why does my house interest them?"

"They want to understand what exactly happened tonight. You're not in any kind of trouble, but people died, and they need to understand exactly what happened, and who did what. It's their job. They'll recreate the scene and go over it a couple times to ensure they have everything nailed down. Their high-powered rifle theory is something that already has them stumped."

"But how can we help them? We didn't see anyone else tonight, and there isn't a rifle at the house," she said.

"That's right. Best thing to do is stick with what we know happened."

Johnny appeared at the doorway. I said goodbye to Jessie and looked at him.

"Who was that?"

"Jessie. She said the doctors think Josh will make it,"

"Thank heavens. She's corroborated everything you said, not that it was necessary. I imagine Josh will, too."

I fought off the irritation made by his comments. "It's the honest truth."

"I believe you, Jim. I really do. However, the kill shot on each of those scumbags out there didn't come from any weapon we've collected so far. You know how we hate unsolved puzzles. It's funny, too, because no one is going to care who put those two down. One of the two had three other smaller holes in him from Josh's or your weapon. He might have died anyway."

"What you're asking me to do is speculate who might have been out there in the field somewhere. A person sitting in the dark night waiting? If Josh wasn't here with me, he might be an obvious choice, but he was here."

"I know," he said.

"She has a lot of friends. Half this town would rally around her. I've seen a handful that I'm sure would do whatever they could to protect her."

"And if someone was out there, like an old boyfriend, they'll never admit to it. One giant goat rope, if you know what I mean," Johnny said, and I did understand.

"He may brag about it one day, but who would prosecute him. The town would give him a medal."

Johnny nodded. "We'll be scrutinizing her security system."

"Please do," I said and grinned. "Give it your best effort."

He raised his hands in defeat. "Put yourself in my shoes," he said and walked outside. A large moth flew by his head and came inside.

I took a step toward the door to close it but realized the large window near it had barely any glass left in it. Xena appeared at the door.

"How's my patient?"

"Fine."

"We're just in the way now. I'm going to be heading home. Do you need a ride? Looks like your car is stuck here for a while?"

"No, I'm fine. Thanks for bandaging my leg, and it was very nice to meet you."

"You, too. Make sure you go to the hospital tomorrow and have your leg looked at. That's an order," she said with a smile and left.

Despite the chattering and occasional laughter outside, the night seemed eerily silent to me. I knew my eardrums were still ringing from all the gunfire. I went into the kitchen and made a cup of coffee with an old one cup Keurig coffee maker. After inspecting the dinner plates that I had moved next to the sink, I picked up the one I thought was mine. Sitting at the kitchen table, I nibbled on what was left of my hamburger and wondered if Jessie had updated the Richardsons.

I sent Jessie a text and suggested she should. She replied with a thumbs up. I didn't know if that meant she did or that she would. Either way, I figured I could move on to other thoughts. She had obviously already talked to her aunt.

A deputy I hadn't met entered the kitchen. "Mr. West, can you come with me. We need to look inside your trunk."

I didn't think they needed to or had any right to, but there was that issue of a missing rifle. Antagonizing them would do no good either. "Sure," I said.

"Should you be eating or drinking that?" he asked as we walked to the car. I ignored him. "I mean this is a crime scene."

"I was eating the hamburger in the kitchen when the dead guys drove up. Nothing related to the crime happened in there, so I couldn't have contaminated anything."

He looked again at my bandaged leg and cut-off jeans. "Were you involved in the shootings?"

I felt like asking him if he was new at this. "Right in the middle."

He suddenly looked impressed. I opened the trunk of my car. He leaned down, sticking his head in, and looked around for a few seconds. He stepped back and said, "Thanks, Mr. West. We're just checking everything off."

"Hey, Jim," Johnny called from a spot next to one of the bodies. He motioned for me to join him as he walked toward a table set up under one of the big lights. Several items, evidence I assumed, were on the table. "Look at this." He pointed at something that I didn't recognize until I got closer. Despite everything and knowing the men were dead, the sight of a machete sent shivers down my spine.

"If I were a betting man, I'd put money on this being the weapon used to murder Perkins, the truck driver. Cobb also had a couple slash wounds, although that's not what killed him," Johnny said.

"I hate to think what they planned on doing with it here. Where was it?"

"We found it partially under one of them. When we turned the lights on, we spotted it. I bet we find old blood traces on it."

"It's a very good thing they won't be able to hurt any more

people. Any idea who they are?" I asked.

"That may have been the easiest step in this whole investigation. From their driver's licenses we found out a lot. They both have criminal records. No one will miss them. They're from Roswell. Not that they'll be going back."

"Want me to stay, or can I head home?"

"Take off. We know how to get in touch. Miss Jessie will be going to her aunt's tonight. We'll have someone here through the night, and some of the guys will come back to look around in daylight tomorrow. Jessie said she and her aunt will come back out tomorrow afternoon."

"I'm afraid what this place will look like in the daylight. A good portion of the front of the house is damaged. That light by the door was only installed a few hours ago. It's trash now," I said.

Before I left, I gave in to a silly impulse to ensure everything that should be was turned off in the house and out back. I started in the kitchen checking the stove and then went to the back porch to check the grill. Other than the lights, which I left on, everything was already off.

Ten minutes later, I maneuvered my Mustang around a handful of police cars that were still there and headed home. I left without my Beretta, part of my jeans, and without eating anything more than a few bites of my hamburger. However, I still had the rifle round I found on the ground next to my car in my pocket. That made me smile.

Chapter 39

The next morning, I decided to close all the loose ends from the day before. I went to the hospital first thing in the morning. The hospital in Clovis is a nice facility, but it has its limitations. They had treated Josh the night before and had kept him alive, but as soon as they could, they helicoptered him to Lubbock, TX, to ensure he stayed alive.

I only had to wait twenty minutes before a nurse and a physician's assistant cleaned my leg wound and stitched it up. The process turned out to be a lot more painful than I had imagined. They twice told me to quit squirming. My whining must have turned them off since I didn't get a lollipop when they were done.

Next, I went to brief Nancy at the donut shop. We had discussed Jessie's situation on more than one occasion, so I thought she would appreciate it. The place was packed with families, but I managed to find a spot to stand at the end of the counter. Nancy joined me a few minutes later.

"Were you involved in all that stuff that went down last night?" she asked. Her expression looked serious and concerned.

"Yes, made me awful hungry for these donuts."

"Don't tease me. I heard on the radio two men were killed, one police officer was critically wounded, and another person suffered a gunshot wound. That other person was you, wasn't it?"

"A minor flesh wound," I said. "More importantly, Jessie is

fine and the bad guys are dead. The other good news is the young deputy should pull through."

"Thank heavens. Are you sure you're okay, Jim?"

"Nothing a few cinnamon cake donuts won't cure."

One of the men working the kitchen called for her, and she left to join him in the kitchen. A little kids soccer team showed up in uniform. There were all smiles and laughter, and I heard one comment about slaughtering the other team. Nancy would have her hands full.

I finished my donuts and walked out, taking the rest of my coffee with me. I received a call from Johnny as I was entering my car. He wanted me to come to his office and provide an official statement. I decided not to put it off and drove directly there.

Interestingly, he had two deputies I had not met interview me. One, a female, who didn't look any older than Josh, might have been at the scene the night before. The other was a much older and out of shape man. His questions gave me the impression he had not been to the scene. The interview was mostly stress-free. At the end, they did try to get me admit that someone else was there with us.

"You should know we've expanded our search out there," the male deputy said.

"What do you mean?"

"We've got a team searching further out. They're looking for anything, you know, shell casings, that kind of stuff."

I stuck to what I knew and what I observed. I refused to speculate, using the same points I had made the night before.

"Jessie has a lot of good friends in Melrose, and anyone of them may have been there hiding in the dark. For all I know, the town may have had a watch list where someone different kept an eye on her house every night. The fact that she might be in danger was obvious to everyone," I said.

The two interviewing me didn't push very hard.

Jessie arrived as I was leaving the building. We talked for a few minutes on the front steps.

"Have you heard any more about Josh?" she asked.

"No, but I see that as good news. How are you doing?"

"Okay. I didn't sleep well, and my aunt kept fussing over me. They want me to give an official statement."

"It's standard procedure. That's why I'm here."

"How did your interview go?"

"Easy. Just stick to what you know, don't speculate. If you don't know an answer to a question, tell them that."

"After I get done here, I'm going to Lubbock. I may spend the night there, but I'll be back tomorrow. I told Bella about last night, and she knows I'll be in Lubbock checking on Josh. She said she may drive over and check on my house. What's left of it, anyway."

"It looks worse than it is," I said.

"I think we were lucky last night, Jim."

"We were. They had us seriously outgunned."

"I think we had a guardian angel."

"Yes, we did."

"I guess I better get inside," she said. She walked away, looking like she had aged ten years overnight. I hoped Josh made a full recovery, and the two of them could return their lives back to what they had.

I drove back to my house wondering when or if Mickie would contact me. I fought the urge to text her. I didn't need confirmation for what I believed happened. Still, I knew the urge to contact her would pester me for the rest of the day.

Chubbs greeted me at the front door.

"Hey, buddy, you seem to be chipper today," I said and led him to the back yard. We played our version of fetch where I threw a tennis ball for him to chase and bring half way back to me. Then he stood next to it barking at me until I walked over to it and tossed it again. We repeated the process several times.

I'm certain his barking, if it could be translated into English would be: "Your turn, fetch!"

My mind kept racing around with memories of the prior night and worries about any fall out from it. I tried to get my mind off it by doing some yard work, but failed. I decided to try my fool-proof method. I went to the golf course.

Being early afternoon, the course wasn't crowded. No matter what occupies my mind when I start a golf round, inevitably I start fixating on my round and what I'm doing wrong. At golf, I'm always doing something wrong.

The second goal I had in going to the golf course had to wait until the back nine. As I walked along a fair-sized lake that had swallowed up dozens of my golf balls over the years, I tossed the rifle round I picked up the night before into the water. I knew the course didn't employ divers to periodically retrieve lost golf balls, and if they ever did, the chances of anyone turning the round over to the police were remote. I hadn't found the second round and hoped no one else would find it either.

Chapter 40

Two months later, Jessie showed up unannounced at my house. I had seen her a few times since the night of the attack, but her arrival surprised me. After we said our hellos, she surprised me again by asking me to take her out to Mickie's.

"She's invited me. She wants to show me how to shoot my gun. Originally, she said to keep it between her and me, but this morning, she said to bring you, too. She somehow knew this was Josh's first day back at work."

"How's he doing?" I asked, although my mind was more curious as to why Mickie wanted to see me. I hadn't had any contact with her since before the attack.

"He's doing great. I mean he still is not a hundred percent, and he'll be on restricted duty, whatever that means, for a while, but he's in good spirits."

"Good."

She stared at me like she was considering whether or not to tell me something. "You know, he asked me to marry him." Her smile when she said this couldn't have gotten any bigger.

"No, I didn't know that. You turned him down, of course," I said, trying to keep my grin hidden.

"No!"

"Congratulations! I was just teasing."

She punched my arm, and then surprised me with a hug.

We left the house a few minutes later in my Mustang, leaving her motorcycle parked on my driveway. Jessie sent a text to

Mickie to tell her we were on our way.

"We haven't set a date yet, but we're looking at early January. You know, ring in the new year with a new husband, a new beginning." She appeared so happy that I couldn't help but share the feeling.

"Have you had much contact with Mickie?" I asked.

"Only a couple of texts. Josh and I had a long conversation about her way back when he was still in the hospital. That conversation took place after he was interviewed by a couple other deputies. The nurse at the hospital said I shouldn't bring up the incident until he was stronger, so I didn't. The interview with the deputies had really upset him."

"Josh brought it up to me. He was very confused at first. He couldn't understand why the other deputies didn't seem to believe him. Josh kept telling them you saved him and killed the two men. They weren't mean to him, but they got Josh agitated, and the doctors asked them to leave. I wasn't there, but he told me about it, and so did a nurse."

"I thought I had killed the two at first, too."

"When he and I discussed everything, he came to the same conclusion we did. Mickie saved us. He wanted to tell his boss right away. We talked a long time, and he finally realized telling on her would cause a lot more harm than good."

"Thanks, I'm glad you did."

"Josh knew Mickie hadn't done anything wrong, at least anything seriously wrong. He had already been shot, and you were, too, before she shot them. That can't be against the law. Plus, I told him Bella was a good shot and could've been the one who saved us just as well. So why tell on Mickie when it could've been Bella."

"I didn't think about her."

"It wasn't her. She would've stuck around to make sure I was okay. Plus, she doesn't like walking around outside at night without a big flashlight. The security camera would've caught the flashlight in the distance. I didn't tell Josh that though." She grinned at me like we were part of a big conspiracy.

"The security cameras caught a lot of what happened out front until the camera and the front light were shot out," I said. I already knew there was no coverage of the two men being hit with the kill shots.

"Afterwards, I took pictures of the front of the house. You know, Jim, kind of like souvenirs. What a mess. Did I tell you that after everything settled down, the town had a really nice fundraiser for me?"

She had, so I nodded. "That was nice of them."

"Oh, one more thing, I was right. It was Shawn who broke into my house that day."

I almost corrected her by saying there was no break-in. She had left a door unlocked.

"After he went back home, and Bella was cleaning up the room he stayed in, she found one of my, well, some of my underwear. She said she called her sister and told her in no uncertain terms that Shawn wouldn't be invited back. She was very mad."

"Was she sure they were yours, not hers?"

Jessie laughed. "Of course."

She continued smiling while we drove down Mickie's driveway. Mickie sat on the porch and stood as we came to a stop. Her dogs stood next to her. Jessie hopped out of the car and hurried toward Mickie. The dogs met her halfway, and the three acted like long lost friends.

I got out a little more cautiously, and one of the dogs took a second from its frolicking to give me the evil eye.

"Come on, Jim. I told Princess that she couldn't eat you today," Mickie laughed as she spoke.

"Princess? More like killer to me." I managed to walk by Jessie and the dogs.

Mickie held out her hand. I shook it. "Thank you," she said softly.

Jessie came up and forced Mickie into a hug. I could see in Mickie's eyes that she didn't want the hug at first but ended up squeezing Jessie back just as hard.

"Thanks," Jessie said.

"For what?"

"For saving us, of course."

"Don't know what you're talking about, but come on in, I've made some iced tea."

Jessie looked at me when Mickie turned her back to lead us into the house. She raised her eyebrows and spread her hands.

"We're better off not knowing for sure." I spoke softly. I don't know if Mickie heard us or not.

Mickie took us straight to the dining room table where she had a pitcher of iced tea and three glasses already waiting for us.

"Thanks for coming over. In addition to our target practice, Jessie, I wanted to bring you both up to speed on some good news."

"Good news is better than bad," I said.

"I was a little worried that even after the two men sent to find the missing necklace were killed, there might be a follow-on effort. However, barely a week after the incident at your house, the necklace was located in Miami. It had never even left the city. Another family member, obviously jealous, stole the necklace to give to his wife."

"All that killing, and it was a family squabble," I said and shook my head.

"Yes, and being family, the thief wasn't killed. They beat him up pretty bad, but that's all. Kind of sad. So, the threat to you, Jessie, is over."

"I already thought it was, but I'm glad to know it really is," Jessie said.

"If you don't mind, Jim, you can go now, and we'll call you when it's time to come back to get Jessie. We need some time for some girl things. You know, talk about weddings and shooting."

I could see Jessie's big grin reappear, and I was used to Mickie's treatment. Mickie walked me out front and surprised me by grabbing ahold of my hand.

"How's your leg?"

"Like new."

"Thank you, Jim." Her eyes stared directly into mine. Her grip on my hand tightened. "Thank you. I let myself get attached to her. If something happened to her, I would've fallen back into that deep pit I never want to be in again. It took me years to get out of it after Afghanistan, and it still wants to draw me back."

"Everything turned out fine, Mickie. You need to keep focused on that, not any what-ifs. Besides, it's me who ought to be thanking you."

"What for?" she asked and walked back into the house.

Chapter 41

In late June, I drove over the pass at Raton, New Mexico, and into Colorado to meet Rose. It had been months since I last saw her, and I was feeling good. I would be picking her up at the airport in Denver. Her plane was scheduled to land in the evening, so we had decided to spend a night in Denver before heading to the small town of Breckenridge. Not as famous as Aspen or Vail, I had always considered the Breckenridge area a lesser-known gem.

Without a doubt, getting to see Rose again brought about my good spirits, but a secondary factor had also eliminated a concern I had had since the night of the attack at Jessie's house. Deputy John Willis had called me the day before to tell me that they were closing the investigation into the attack.

"We're closing the books on this one," he said to me on the phone. "It's only been open this long because we were trying to find some evidence that might identify our missing shooter. We hate loose ends."

"No luck?"

"No. Never could find any spent rounds, or shell casings, or anything else for that matter. Plenty of animal tracks and burrows, but nothing that helped."

"All that open land, I imagine it was like looking for a needle in a haystack."

"Yes, the experts told me the round that took out a portion of the one guy's face could've gone on to travel a long distance. It could also have been deflected, but not knowing where it originated, being deflected didn't matter. However, the other round, the through and through, shouldn't have travelled far, but we couldn't find it. That one's a puzzle," he said.

I imagined that round was the one I found. It was now sitting at the bottom of the lake on the golf course next to dozens of my golf balls.

"And no one ever came forward to say anything?"

"No, the whole town wants to give the person a medal. They don't want to turn him in. Can't say I blame them."

I almost said "him or her" in response to his comment no one wanted to turn him in. Instead, I smiled and kept that comment to myself.

The last of the clouds in the sky disappeared as I approached Trinidad. It was going to be a wonderful day.

Title: *Dead Men Can Kill*™
Author: Bob Doerr
Publisher: TotalRecall Publications, Inc.
Paper Back: ISBN: 978-1-59095-759-2
eBook: ISBN: 978-1-59095-761-5
Number of pages: 320
Publication: 2009

When Jim West, a former Air Force Special Agent with the Office of Special Investigations, moves back to New Mexico, his goal is simple: start an easy going second career as a professional lecturer on investigative techniques to colleges and civic organizations. He never envisioned that his practical demonstration of forensic hypnosis on stage with a state university student would stir up memories of an 18-year old murder mystery. When the student is murdered three days later, West finds himself ensnared in a web of intrigue that pits him and the small town's authorities against a ruthless, psychotic killer.

An aggressive reporter for the town newspaper seeks out West for help with the story, but after one of her co-workers is murdered, she quickly aligns her efforts with West and the Sheriff. As West works closely with her, he begins to wonder if this could be the first real relationship for him since his devastating divorce a few years earlier.

The killer, though, has other plans for the reporter and the story takes fascinating twists and turns, leading to an inevitable, riveting confrontation.

Look out for a new hero on the mystery/thriller landscape! Jim West, retired military investigator, is resourceful, intuitive, pragmatic and always competent. All of West's abilities are tested when he matches wits with psychopathic serial killer William White, a man whose appreciation for murder is surpassed only by his delight in domination. Bob Doerr has crafted a must-read addition to the genre in Dead Men Can Kill, which evolves from absorbing story to absolute page-turner as West closes in on a killer who is supposedly dead. Highly recommended!

--Dallin Malmgren, author of...
The Whole Nine Yards The Ninth Issue Is This for a Grade?

A Jim West™ Mystery/Thriller Book 1

Title: *Cold Winter's Kill*™
Author: Bob Doerr
Publisher: TotalRecall Publications, Inc.
Paper Back: ISBN: 978-1-59095-763-9
eBook: ISBN: 978-1-59095-764-6
Number of pages: 288
Publication: 2009

Cold Winter's Kill is a fast-paced thriller that takes place in the scenic mountains of Lincoln County, New Mexico and throws Jim West into a race against time to stop a psychopath who abducts and kills a young blonde every Christmas...

It was one of those phone calls former Air Force Special Agent Jim West never wanted to receive--an old friend calling to ask if he could drive down to Ruidoso, New Mexico to help locate his daughter who has disappeared while on a ski trip with friends. Jim found himself heading to Ruidoso even though he believed, much like the local authorities, that if she had gone missing in the mountains in December, her survival chances were slim. He didn't want to be there when they found her, but still he drove on.

Once in Ruidoso, Jim discovers a sinister coincidence that changes everything. It appears that someone is abducting and killing one young blond every year around Christmas. The race is on--can Jim locate his friend's daughter in time? But why is this happening and who's doing it?

Jim can't wait for the local authorities to raise the priority of their search, or for the pending blizzard to pass. In his haste he puts himself in the killer's sights. Will he, too, suffer from a cold winter's kill?

"GREAT SUSPENSE! In *Cold Winter's Kill* Bob Doerr grabs your attention from the beginning and holds it until the last sentence. Hard to put down!"
    --Shelba Nicholson
    former Women's Editor, *Texarkana Gazette*

A Jim West™ Mystery/Thriller Book 2

Title: *Loose Ends Kill*™
Author: Bob Doerr
Publisher: TotalRecall Publications, Inc.
Paper Back: ISBN: 978-1-59095-718-9
eBook: ISBN: 978-1-59095-719-6
Number of pages: 288
Publication: 2010

    LOOSE ENDS KILL **is a fast-paced mystery/thriller** that takes place in the historic city of San Antonio, Texas, and throws Jim West into the middle of a police investigation of the murder of an old friend's wife. The police already believe they have the killer in custody – West's friend.

    West is drawn into this mystery by a call from the old friend who requests his assistance. West agrees to help his friend and digs deep to try to find another suspect. In the process he soon discovers that he is being followed and targeted for harassment, but by whom?

    West quickly discovers that he didn't know his old friend's wife as well as he thought. To his surprise, he learns that she has had a number of affairs dating back for more than a decade. In fact, while investigating the murder, he realizes that his friend and he may be the only two people unaware of her philandering behavior.

    Theorizing that one of her lovers could have had just as much motive as her husband, West starts turning over the rocks identifying one lover after another. In doing so, West unintentionally ignites an outbreak of more death and mayhem. The police and his friend's lawyers want West to go back home. The police even threaten to arrest him.

    Soon, West believes the real killer wants him gone or dead. Deciding the only way to resolve the case before the outside pressures force him to leave, he sets a trap for the killer using himself as bait. However, he soon learns he may have only outsmarted himself.

A Jim West™ Mystery/Thriller Book 3

Title: *Another Colorado Kill*™

Author: Bob Doerr

Publisher: TotalRecall Publications, Inc.

Paper Back: ISBN: 978-1-59095-785-1

eBook: ISBN: 978-1-59095-786-8

Number of pages: 288

Publication Date: 2011

It was supposed to be a short, fun golf outing, but when Jim West and his friend Edward "Perry" Mason stumble across a dead body in a restroom at a rest stop along I-25, things turn bad and then only get worse.

With the golf outing shot, West intends to stay in Colorado Springs only for a day or two. However, when two more murder victims turn up – one with West's name handwritten in her notebook - the heat on West skyrockets. The police instruct him to stick around, and soon he discovers that while the police may want to pin the crimes on him, the killer wants him out of the picture. Way out – like dead.

West's only ally is Lieutenant Michelle Prado, a tall red head with large green eyes that captivate West. Assigned to keep an eye on West, Lieutenant Prado decides the best way to do so is to keep him close. West and Prado do their own digging into the investigation. In the process, Jim wonders how close their relationship will evolve.

It seems to West that as the police focus less on him, the killer intensifies his focus on him. Barely surviving an initial confrontation, West realizes he must take the initiative. If he doesn't, or perhaps even if he does - he may end up as just another Colorado kill.

A Jim West™ Mystery/Thriller Book 4

Title: *No One Else To Kill*™
Author: Bob Doerr
Publisher: TotalRecall Publications, Inc.
Paper Back: ISBN: 978-1-59095-423-2
eBook: ISBN: 978-1-59095-424-9
Number of pages: 352
Publication Date: 2012

No One Else to Kill, **Bob Doerr, TotalRecall Publications** - In this newest book in the popular Jim West series, Mr. West finds himself stood up and out of town. Looking forward to some R & R he keeps his reservation at the remote hunting lodge. Located in the Pecos Wilderness area in New Mexico it's a hunter's haven. Expecting to do nothing other than relax, he has no idea what the rest of the weekend holds for him. When a murder takes place, the hotel guest are detained and no one is beyond suspicion. The sheriff is called in, and while the investigation is underway, a second murder takes place. Both crimes are clearly related, but by whom and why? With time running out and unable to find a motive, the legal experts seek Jim's help.

2013
Eric Hoffer Award
WINNER
Excellence in
Independent
Publishing

2013
da Vinci Eye
FINALIST
Eric Hoffer Award
Excellence in
Independent Publishing

The cover for *No One Else To Kill* is a 2013 finalist for the da Vinci Eye award.

Bob's four previous novels in the series are titled *Dead Men Can Kill, Cold Winter's Kill, Loose Ends Kill,* and *Another Colorado Kill.* The latter two were selected as Eric Hoffer Award finalists for 2010 and 2011, respectively.

Bob Doerr's *No One Else To Kill* was awarded the Grand Prize in the "Books With Out Publishers" writing contest at www.ultimateherocontest.com

A Jim West™ Mystery/Thriller Book 5

Title: *Caffeine Can Kill*™

Author: Bob Doerr

Publisher: TotalRecall Publications, Inc.

Paper Back: ISBN: 978-1-59095-562-8

eBook: ISBN: 978-1-59095-563-5

Number of pages: 240

Publication Date: 2017

This Jim West mystery/thriller, the sixth in the series, finds Jim traveling to the Texas Hill Country to attend the grand opening of a friend's winery and vineyard. Upon arriving in Fredericksburg, Jim witnesses a brutal kidnapping at a local coffee shop. The next morning while driving down an unpaved country road to the grand opening, he comes across an active crime scene barely a quarter mile from his friend's winery. A Fredericksburg policeman who talked to Jim the day before at the kidnapping scene recognizes Jim and asks him to identify the body of a dead young woman as the woman who was kidnapped. Jim does, and as a result of this unwelcome relationship with the police is asked the next morning to identify the body of another murdered person as the man who had kidnapped the young woman. A third murder throws Jim's vacation into complete disarray and draws Jim and a female friend into the sights of one of the killers.

A Jim West™ Mystery/Thriller Book 6

Title: *Greed Can Kill*™
Author: Bob Doerr
Publisher: TotalRecall Publications, Inc.
Paper Back: ISBN: 978-1-59095-731-8
eBook: ISBN: 978-1-59095-741-7
Number of pages: 280
Publication Date: 2017

This adventure finds Jim traveling to Fabens, TX, in an effort to locate an old acquaintance who had written Jim a cryptic letter asking for his help in finding a briefcase. In Fabens, he discovers that someone has murdered his friend. Jim provides a copy of the letter to the local police explaining that he has no idea where the briefcase is or how to decipher the sets of numbers provided in the letter. Figuring there is nothing more he can do, Jim starts his trek back home. He plans to spend a night or two relaxing at the Lodge in Cloudcroft, NM, on his way only to find that he is being followed. An ominous, unidentified phone caller gives Jim an ultimatum - find the briefcase and turn it over to him within a week.

A violent confrontation in Cloudcroft verifies Jim's worst suspicion, a Mexican drug cartel wants the briefcase. The confrontation also brings the FBI into the picture. They also want Jim to continue his search. The search takes Jim to the New Mexican ghost town of Chloride where the final confrontation takes place and Jim finds out who the bad guys really are.

A Jim West™ Mystery/Thriller Book 7

Title: *Honeymoons Can Kill*™
Author: Bob Doerr
Publisher: TotalRecall Publications, Inc.
Paper Back: ISBN: 978-1-59095-314-3
eBook: ISBN: 978-1-59095-518-5
Number of pages: 270
Publication Date: 2020

Honeymoons Can Kill is a 68,000 word mystery thriller that is set on a cruise ship in the Gulf of Mexico. The eighth book in the Jim West series, this is the first book to bring back prior characters from previous books. Deputy Rose Luna (Greed Can Kill) joins Jim on a five day cruise out of Galveston, TX, and on the second day of the cruise, the couple encounters Sarah Stone (Dead Men Can Kill). Sarah Stone is now Sarah Lassiter having gotten married on the ship right before it left port. When Sarah's new husband is murdered on the second night of the cruise, the cruise changes from a relaxing vacation to a race to catch the killer before everyone disembarks in three more days. The book should be considered as rated PG-13.

A Jim West™ Mystery/Thriller Book 8

Title: *Double Bogeys Can Kill*™

Author: Bob Doerr

Publisher: TotalRecall Publications, Inc.

Paper Back: ISBN: 978-1-64883-166-9

eBook: ISBN: 978-1-64883-167-6

Number of pages: 238

Publication Date: 2022

Double Bogeys Can Kill is the 9th Jim West mystery/thriller. In this book West finds himself in Myrtle Beach joining 15 retired air force pilots, to fill a void and allow the group to have four foursomes. The week, usually fun and something the pilots look forward to, quickly turns into tragedy as one of the golfers is murdered after the first day of golf. The pilots know West's background as a criminal investigator in the air force and lean on him to solve the murder. The Myrtle Beach police also learn of West's background and want him to be their inside man. West doesn't want the role, knowing it's a lose-lose proposition. He's right, and on the second night, the murderer seeing West as a threat tries to kill him. West survives but requires a trip to the hospital. The suspect pool shrinks down to his fellow golfers. Balancing his cooperation with the police with his golf is not easy as the whole group starts to turn on itself. Finally, West is confronted by the killer now crazy enough to kill himself and take West with him.

A Jim West™ Mystery/Thriller Book 9

Title: *Curiosity Can Kill*™

Author: Bob Doerr

Publisher: TotalRecall Publications, Inc.

Paper Back: ISBN: 978-1-64883-340-3

eBook: ISBN: 978-1-64883-341-0

Number of pages: 280

Publication Date: 2024

West travels to Alpine, Texas, to help a friend's widow identify the body of her husband. He was killed in Big Bend National Park, more accurately described as the middle of nowhere. When a second person is murdered at the same spot, and the widow is then murdered, things really get strange. Jim is drawn into a hunt for the killer. Oh, and did somebody mention demons?

A Jim West™ Mystery/Thriller Book 10

PUBLIC SAFETY WRITERS ASSOCIATION
WRITING COMPETITION

Non-Published Fiction Book
First Place
Bob Doerr
for
Curiosity Can Kill

PUBLIC
SAFETY

July 13, 2024

WRITERS
ASSOCIATION

Title: *The Attack*™
Author: Bob Doerr
Publisher: TotalRecall Publications, Inc.
Paper Back: ISBN: 978-1-59095-146-0
eBook: ISBN: 978-1-59095-147-7
Number of pages: 286
Publication Date: 2014

A terrorist team has just set off four explosive devices in an international airport close to New York City. The leader of the terrorists, Ahmad Khalin, survives the attack and plans to attack a second U.S. airport within the month. As Khalin makes his escape from the New York area he is involved in a shooting in Connecticut. Clint Smith, a U.S. government agent assigned to an ultra-secret agency, is at a restaurant across the street when the shooting occurs. He responds to the scene to see if he can help, but Khalin is gone. On a hunch, Teresa Deer, Smith's boss, sends Smith after Khalin. Smith's pursuit takes him to Bar Harbor, Maine; Wiesbaden, Germany; the Costa Brava, Spain; Northern Scotland; Lake of the Woods, Ontario, Canada; and finally into Saskatchewan, Canada, where the final confrontation takes place. Throughout the pursuit, a number of interesting characters add to the subplots and try to survive their involvement in the chase.

A Clint Smith Thriller™

Title: *The Group*™
Author: Bob Doerr
Publisher: TotalRecall Publications, Inc.
Paper Back: ISBN: 978-1-59095-569-7
eBook: ISBN: 978-1-59095-570-3
Number of pages: 288
Publication Date: 2016

A fast-moving international thriller that pits a lone government operative, known as a hunter, against an unknown group of assassins who pose a worldwide threat.

Someone is killing off the world's rich and famous. The murders are sophisticated, requiring precision and skill. The international community is in an uproar but has no leads in its attempt to find the assassins. The victims were members of the Bilderberg Group, an international, loose knit group of the uber rich that meet annually. While the attacks have not had a direct impact on the U.S., Theresa Deer, Director of the Special Section, a small unit whose existence is known by only a handful in the U.S. government, sees this new age League of Assassins as a national threat. She sends her hunters out. Clint Smith finds their trail Switzerland where his discovery almost leads to his own death. The hunt leads him to Mallorca, Spain, where he witnesses a helicopter attack on a villa where a number of attendees from the Bilderberg conference were holding a follow-on meeting of their own. Smith picks up the trail a couple weeks later in Las Vegas, NV, and in his hunt finds out that he is no longer the hunter. He has become the prey.

A Clint Smith Thriller™

Title: *The Assassins*™
Author: Bob Doerr
Publisher: TotalRecall Publications, Inc.
Paper Back: ISBN: 978-1-59095-196-5
eBook: ISBN: 978-1-59095-197-2
Number of pages: 240
Publication Date: 2018

A disputed election has divided the nation, and a handful of senior government officials have conspired to have the North Koreans assassinate the President of the United States. Believing the assassination attempt to be only days away, Theresa Deer, Director of the Special Section, a small unit whose existence is known by only a few in the U.S. government, is tasked to interdict the man intent on providing the North Koreans vital information about the president's itinerary for his visit to South Korea. While Deer succeeds in her mission, she is severely injured and finds herself being hunted by the North Korean assassins. Clint Smith is sent to Korea to help Deer get back to the U.S. and finds himself caught in a deadly game of cat and mouse with the North Koreans. With no one in the U.S. government to turn to for help, and the South Koreans now also hunting them, getting out of South Korea alive is looking unlikely.

A Clint Smith Thriller™

Title: *The Treasure*™

Author: Bob Doerr

Publisher: TotalRecall Publications, Inc.

Paper Back: ISBN: 978-1-64883-084-6

eBook: ISBN: 978-1-64883-085-3

Number of pages: 242

Publication Date: 2021

The Treasure is the fourth book in the Clint Smith thriller series. After a successful mission in South America, Clint heads to Las Vegas on vacation and to dig up a stagecoach strong box he had found in the desert earlier but had not opened. Upon inspection, he finds some old gold coins in mint condition and some well-preserved documents. He gives the contents of the strong box to a lawyer to find buyers. One of the documents, unfortunately, creates a maelstrom of violence and murder, and puts Clint squarely in the cross hairs of some Chinese assassins. Clint leaves Las Vegas to keep out of the spotlight, only to find himself going to Alaska in an attempt to rescue a female police officer who had been assigned to protect him in Las Vegas.

A Clint Smith Thriller™

Title: *The Scientists*™

Author: Bob Doerr

Publisher: TotalRecall Publications, Inc.

Paper Back: ISBN: 978-1-64883-328-1

eBook: ISBN: 978-1-64883-329-8

Number of pages: 234

Publication Date: 2024

This is the 5ᵗʰ Clint Smith novel. Clint is a hunter, a government assassin, employed by a very small, ultra secret agency. Someone has been kidnapping scientists from various countries. All are tops in their field and experts in the modernization of drones. As the world's security and intelligence services make little progress in solving the disappearances, Clint is put on alert. Three separate drone attacks occur, resulting in a number of deaths. Once the lethal drones are perfected, the kidnapped scientists' usefulness comes to an end. While Clint's mission does not include rescue, he's given the green light to go after his target. His success may prevent some of them from dying. Time is tight and the enemy is no pushover, but the game is on.

A Clint Smith Thriller™

Title: *The Enchanted Coin*™

Author: Bob Doerr

Publisher: TotalRecall Publications, Inc.

Paper Back: ISBN: 978-1-59095-084-5

eBook: ISBN: 978-1-59095-085-2

Audible Book Available: ASIN B01C4SVOOQ

Number of pages: 130

Publication Date: 2013

We have all heard of tales of UFO's, ghosts, people who say they can talk to the spirits, ancient curses, and magical talismans. Most of us automatically dismiss them as false, figments of people's imagination, and understandably so. However, might not just a few of them be true? I don't know, but I heard this story from a young man the other day who swore the fascinating tale I have set forth in this book really did really occur, because it happened to him. You be the judge.

Title: *The Rescue of Vincent*™

Author: Bob Doerr

Publisher: TotalRecall Publications, Inc.

Paperback, ISBN: 978-1-59095-279-5

eBook: ISBN: 978-1-59095-280-1

Audible Book Available: ASIN B01FYCPML0

Number of pages: 160

Publication Date: 2014

The Rescue of Vincent: Book 2 in The Enchanted Coin Series is a 31,000 word fantasy adventure targeted at Middle Grade readers. Imagine being a fourteen year old again and finding a coin that seems to give off a light of its own. The coin has your name on it, and instructs you to toss it into a fountain next to the Tree of Life. That's what happens in *The Rescue of Vincent*, and what starts my protagonist off on a magical adventure that many young boys and girls would love to have. This book is "G" rated.

Title: *The Magic of Vex*™
Author: Bob Doerr
Publisher: TotalRecall Publications, Inc.
Paper Back: ISBN: 978-1-59095-309-9
eBook: ISBN: 978-1-59095-280-1
Audible Book Available: ASIN B01G7NQCD2
Number of pages: 140
Publication Date: 2015

Samantha Gillespie's discovery of a magic coin results in her transportation to the strange world of Vex where magic is real and where she has to over-come a number of challenges if she ever hopes to return home.

What happened to Samantha was totally unexpected and quite frightening. It led her to an adventure that many might think impossible to believe, but it did. You be the judge.

This book is "G" rated.

Title: *Stranded in Space* ™
Author: Bob Doerr
Publisher: TotalRecall Publications, Inc.
Paper Back: ISBN: 978-1-59095-418-8
eBook: ISBN: 978-1-59095-419-5
Number of pages: 152
Publication Date: 2022

Stranded in Space: Book 4 in The Enchanted Coin Series is a 31,000 word fantasy adventure targeted at Middle Grade readers. Imagine being a fourteen year old again and finding a coin that seems to give off a light of its own. The coin has your name on it, claims to be magical, and instructs you to toss it into a fountain next to the Tree of Life. That's what happens in Stranded in Space, and what starts my protagonist off on a magical adventure that many young boys and girls would love to have. You be the judge.

This book is "G" rated.

Titles by Bob Doerr

Jim West mystery/thriller™ Series
Dead Men Can Kill™
Cold Winters Kill™
Another Colorado Kill™
Loose Ends Kill™
No One Else To Kill™
Caffeine Can Kill™
Greed Can Kill™
Honeymoons Can Kill™
Double Bogeys Can Kill™
Curiosity Can Kill™
A Dark Shadow's Kill™

A Clint Smith Thriller™ Series
The Attack™
The Group™
The Assassins™
The Treasure™
The Scientists™

Mouse Gate™ Series
The Enchanted Coin™
The Rescue of Vincent™
The Magic of Vex™
Stranded in Space™

Author Bob Doerr Uses his special knowledge
to provide authentic details in his novels
about how law enforcement agencies do their work.

For a complete list of books by Bob Doerr,
a preview of upcoming titles and more
visit his website.
www.bobdoerr.com

www.ingramcontent.com/pod-product-compliance
Lightning Source LLC
Chambersburg PA
CBHW020626110726
47899CB00002B/671